a
Tangled
Wreath

a tangled wreath

LAURA BEERS

Text copyright © 2021 by Laura Beers
Cover art copyright © 2021 by Laura Beers

All rights reserved. No part of this publication may be reproduced, stored, copied, or transmitted without the prior written permission of the copyright owner. This is a work of fiction. Names, characters, places and incidents either are the product of the author's imagination or are used fictitiously. Any resemblance to actual persons, living or dead, business establishments, events, or locales is entirely coincidental.

Dear Margarette

Langdon Hall, Maidstone
December 1, 1815

My cherished friend, can you believe that Christmastide is almost upon us? It is a time that I cherish deeply, even more since my beloved Henry died so long ago. He used to follow me around with mistletoe until I gave him a proper kiss. How I miss him! I never thought my heart would recover from losing him, but your friendship has bolstered me over these years.

I must admit that I look forward to every letter I receive here, especially since we are not spending Christmas together. Perhaps I can host a house party when the weather is agreeable, and we can all sit around and play whist. Wouldn't that be grand?

You mustn't fret about me, because I am fortunate enough to have my granddaughter, Arabella, visiting for the holiday. You may have heard the news around Town, but her fiancé broke off their engagement, leaving her utterly devastated. Frankly, I am pleased. I never did care for Lord Eastwood. He is entirely too vain and pretentious for my liking. I'm not quite sure what Arabella ever saw in him, especially since he is a known rake amongst the *ton*. But I am just the grandmother, and I was forced to bite my tongue for Arabella's sake.

Even so, I refuse to sit back and do nothing but watch my granddaughter suffer. I know just the man who will solve all of Arabella's problems. I hope I am not just being foolish, but I do worry about her. She doesn't deserve the poor treatment she has received. I have already come up with the perfect ruse to bring these two together.

I do hope I am successful at playing matchmaker. You inspired all of us to try our hand at it, and the prospect has given me such hope. I heard that Euota and Eugenia even have a friendly wager in place. Have you heard from them?

Arabella is stubborn and I know she will fight this, but I do so desperately want her to be happy. I have also recruited my dear friend Lady Barrett to help with the scheme. Do you remember her? She is a dear woman who has had much tragedy befall her, as well.

I am counting down the days until Arabella arrives and we can start up this scheme. I feel slightly giddy at the thought of bringing together two people who are destined to be with one another. With any luck, I shall see my great grandchildren before I die. Is that selfish of me? Perhaps, but I am old, and no one can fault me for that.

I do look forward to receiving your letter and hearing your thoughts on the matter. It shall be a Christmas unlike any other, I can assure you of that.

Fondly yours,
Esther

Chapter One

Lady Arabella Wyndham stared out the window of the coach as it rolled through the countryside. She was traveling to her grandmother's house to spend Christmas with her, and she hoped a change of scenery would do her good. Frankly, she wasn't sure what would help her now, especially since her reputation was in tatters due to not one, but two broken engagements.

What had become of her? She once was a diamond of the first water, but that all changed after her first broken engagement with Lord Barrett. He had called off the engagement to serve in the Royal Army, shattering her heart in the process. She had been young, naïve, and never thought any misfortune would fall upon her. How foolish she had been. Since then, she had guarded her heart, not allowing anyone in.

Arabella hoped she would find some solace at her grandmother's estate. She needed a respite from her unrelenting thoughts, knowing she was destined for spinsterhood. She was tired of pretending all was well when her life was crumbling around her, threatening to consume every last ounce of joy.

Her lady's maid, Mary, spoke up. "Are you all right, milady?"

"I am," Arabella lied, bringing her gaze back to meet hers.

Mary didn't appear convinced but fortunately didn't press her. "How much longer until we arrive at Lady Langdon's country home?"

"It shouldn't be much longer," Arabella replied. "I do appreciate you coming along with me. It has made the trip much more bearable."

"You don't have to keep thanking me for doing my job."

"But I feel as if I must, since I am taking you away from your family on Christmas."

Mary gave a slight shrug of her shoulders. "We shall celebrate once I return."

Arabella found herself envious of her lady's maid and her close-knit family. It was something she wished she possessed. Her father had recently married a woman only five years older than herself, and the woman was truly awful to her. When she complained to her father about her stepmother's ill treatment towards her, he just dismissed her out of hand.

The coach turned down the lane that led to her grandmother's country home, and she admired the trees that lined the road. They had grown since the last time she had visited Langdon Hall nearly five years ago. She hadn't been back here since that fateful day when Lord Barrett had visited her for the last time.

The coach stopped in front of a large, rectangular manor with a portico over the main door. After the footman stepped off the perch and placed the step down, he opened the door and assisted them out of the coach.

Arabella stared up at Langdon Hall and attempted to fight back the flood of unwelcome memories that came to her mind. She wasn't here to relive the past, but to learn how to move forward. She was still rooted in her spot when the main door opened and she was greeted by a familiar face.

"Good evening," Moore said, opening the door wide.

She smiled at the aging butler as she approached him. He

A Tangled Wreath

was short, with white, thinning hair, and his shoulders were hunched over. "It is good to see you looking so well," she replied before she stepped into the entry hall.

"I daresay that you need spectacles, milady," he joked. "I am a withered old man."

"I'm afraid I do not see you that way."

Moore closed the door behind her and shared, "Your grandmother has been rather anxious for your arrival all day."

"Is that so?"

"I caught Lady Langdon, on more than a few occasions, glancing out of the window to see if your coach had arrived," Moore revealed.

Her grandmother's voice came from the doorway to the drawing room. "It is true," she admitted. "I was anxious to see my favorite granddaughter."

"I am your only granddaughter."

"It makes you no less my favorite," her grandmother said, opening her arms wide.

Arabella hurried over and embraced her. It felt good to be wrapped up in loving arms, and she allowed herself to linger.

Her grandmother released her and stepped back. "How are you, my child?"

"I am well."

"We both know that is not true."

"Why do you say that?"

"Because Lord Eastwood was an idiot to break your engagement."

"I would concur."

Her grandmother turned her attention towards Moore. "We will require some refreshment in the drawing room," she said. "Furthermore, Lady Arabella will require a bath. Will you see to the heating of the water?"

Moore tipped his head. "Yes, milady."

"Follow me," her grandmother ordered as she spun on her heel.

Arabella followed her into the drawing room and joined her on the settee. Her grandmother's silver hair was pulled back into a tight chignon, emphasizing the deep lines on her face.

"How was your journey?" her grandmother asked.

"Uneventful."

Her grandmother nodded in approval. "Those are generally the best kind of journeys."

"I would have much rather been stopped by a highwayman."

"Good heavens, why would you want that?"

"It might have helped with my humdrum."

Her grandmother's face softened. "You have had a rough go of it, haven't you?"

"I have," Arabella admitted, "and I am not entirely sure it will get much better."

"It will."

"How can you be so sure?"

Reaching forward, her grandmother patted her leg. "You must trust me on this," she said. "I have seen a few things in my years."

"I do trust you, but I fear that I am a lost cause."

"No one is a lost cause," her grandmother asserted.

A tray was delivered, and her grandmother poured and extended a cup of tea.

"Thank you," Arabella said, accepting the offering.

Her grandmother took a long sip of her own tea before asking, "How is your father doing?"

Arabella huffed. "My father seems quite taken by his new wife, but I find Augusta to be rather vexing."

"How so?"

"Augusta and I were never on friendly terms, but our animosity towards one another has only continued to grow since she has become my stepmother," Arabella shared. "She

A Tangled Wreath

was able to convince my father that I would be more comfortable in another area of the townhouse."

"Are you?"

Arabella shook her head. "No, I find the room to be rather drafty."

"Then why didn't you stand up for yourself?"

"It isn't that easy," Arabella argued. "My father has fallen under Augusta's spell and agrees with everything she says."

"That must be frustrating."

"It is, especially since my mother has only been dead for six months now," Arabella said. "How could he have moved on so quickly?"

Her grandmother took a sip of her tea. "It was rather sudden, but I'm afraid it is commonplace for gentlemen to remarry quickly."

"I can't help but wonder if he only married Augusta to sire a son."

"Your father does need an heir."

Arabella glanced down at her teacup. "I have no doubt that my father is disappointed that I wasn't born a boy."

"Your father loves you."

Arabella sniffed. "I am not entirely sure that is true," she responded. "He sent me away so he could celebrate Christmas with Augusta."

"That was my doing," her grandmother stated. "I asked your father if you could come and keep me company for Christmas."

"You could have always joined us in Town."

"I'm afraid my withered bones detest long carriage rides."

"You are not that old, Grandmother."

"I wish that were the case, but I can tweak my back just by leaning over wrong."

Arabella gave her an amused smile. "Regardless, you would have traveled to Town to come to my wedding."

"I would have, but I correctly assumed that Lord Eastwood would break the engagement."

"How could you have known that?"

With a knowing look, her grandmother asked, "Did you ever post the banns?"

"No, we did not," Arabella replied. "Herbert kept prolonging the engagement."

"Which isn't normal, my dear."

"I know, but I had little choice in the matter," Arabella sighed. "I didn't dare break off the engagement with him."

Her grandmother's brow lifted. "Did you even love him?"

Arabella shifted uncomfortably in her seat, delaying her response. "I cared for him, but, no, I did not love him."

"Why did you even agree to the engagement, then?"

"It would have been an advantageous marriage since he will be a marquess one day," she replied.

Her grandmother leaned forward and placed her teacup on the tray. "I, for one, am glad that Lord Eastwood ended it."

"How can you say that?" Arabella asked, unable to keep the disbelief out of her voice. "I am ruined now, and I have no doubt that I will become a spinster."

"You mustn't give up hope."

Arabella frowned. "I'm afraid I am past hope," she replied. "Two broken engagements are not something the *ton* is willing to overlook."

Moore stepped into the room and met her gaze. "Your bath is readied, milady, and your lady's maid is ready to assist you," he informed her.

"Thank you," Arabella replied. "I shall be right up."

"Why don't you go enjoy a long soak," her grandmother suggested as the butler left, "and we shall continue this conversation later."

"I would prefer it if we didn't." Arabella set her teacup on the tray as she rose. "Some things are better left unsaid."

Her grandmother gave her a compassionate look. "I know

you believe your future is bleak, but I can assure you that is not the case."

Arabella disagreed, but chose to retreat rather than argue. "It would be best if I adjourn to my bedchamber while the water is warm."

"Go enjoy your soak," her grandmother encouraged.

Arabella exited the drawing room, tears pricking at the back of her eyes, but she blinked them away. Her life was in shambles, and no one could help her now.

COLIN NOTLEY, the Earl of Barrett, was utterly miserable. He was tired of the monotony of his life. It felt as if he did the same thing every blasted day. He had been happy serving in the Royal Army, finding purpose in serving "for King and Country". That had been taken away when his older brother, Paul, tragically died in a boating accident. Colin had inherited, and now his days were filled with meetings and reviewing ledgers.

He stared out of his bedchamber window to the expansive gardens below. With Paul's passing, he had inherited an earldom and more money than he could spend in a lifetime. But this was not how he wanted his life to be. He felt trapped, and he saw no way out of it.

He knew he had no right to complain, especially since he had a life that most would be envious of. But his wealth came with great responsibility. Not only did his servants rely on him for their livelihood, but he had hundreds of tenants who lived on his lands.

His valet's voice broke through his musings. "Are you thinking of running off to join the army again?"

"How did you know?" Colin asked, turning to face the man.

Simon smiled. "You insult me, my lord," he said. "I served

with you for nearly five years as your batman, and I believe I know you fairly well."

"That is true."

Simon held up two cravats for his inspection. "Which one would you care to wear today?"

"Those are identical."

"Not so," Simon replied. "One is white, and the other is ivory."

Colin waved his hand in front of him. "Just pick one."

Simon set one of the cravats on the bed and returned the other to the armoire. "Do you have any thoughts on the selection of your waistcoat today?"

"Just pick any blasted waistcoat," Colin grumbled.

"I see that you are in a pleasant mood this morning," Simon said lightly, removing a green waistcoat from the armoire. "Is there a particular reason why?"

"I should be out in the field with my regiment, but I am stuck here at my estate," Colin said.

"Some might consider you fortunate."

"I am not one of them."

Simon held open the waistcoat. "You fought valiantly against Napoleon and were one of the lucky ones to survive."

"I should have died alongside my men," Colin asserted, turning to insert his arms into the garment. "Instead, I lived, but so many of my comrades died."

"It is not your fault that those men died."

Colin rubbed his left leg where a bullet was still lodged. "I could have done more."

"You were injured—"

Colin cut him off. "It matters not."

Simon gave him a condoling look. "You are being much too hard on yourself, sir," he said. "You were near death when the medics found you among the casualties."

Colin walked over to the bed and picked up his blue

jacket. "They should have fixed me up and sent me on my way."

"You know very well they couldn't do that," Simon remarked as he wordlessly took the jacket and replaced it with the cravat. "Wellington received orders that you were to be on the next ship home."

Walking over to the mirror, Colin began tying his cravat. "Rather than dealing with what truly matters, I am resolving petty disputes amongst my tenants."

"It does matter," Simon attempted. "You employ hundreds of people and have even more tenants on your land. Without you, what would become of them?"

Colin dropped his hands to his side. "I have no doubt that they would survive."

"I can't help but wonder if your mother is right," Simon said as he assisted Colin into the jacket.

"About what, precisely?" Colin asked, warily.

"Perhaps it is time for you to take a bride."

Colin tensed under the brush Simon was using. "I have no plans to marry."

"May I ask why that is?"

"No, you may not."

Simon tipped his head. "I apologize if I offended you," he said. "That was not my intention."

"Some people are destined to be alone, and I am one of those people."

"You don't have to be."

"I deserve to be."

Simon eyed him curiously. "Why do you say that?"

"It hardly matters," Colin replied curtly, opening the door. "I'm afraid I am late for a meeting with my gamekeeper."

Colin didn't wait for his valet's response before he headed into the hall. There was only one young woman he would ever consider marrying, but she was already engaged to another. Not that he blamed her; Lady Arabella deserved better than how he treated her. He'd never intended to fall in love with her, but he had, desperately. He still carried a miniature portrait of her in his jacket pocket.

But she had moved on. He was grateful for it. He was not the man he once was, and he knew he could never make her happy. He was too ragged from his service in the army.

As Colin descended the stairs, his butler approached him with a smile on his face. "Good morning, milord," Dickson said in a cheery voice. "I trust that you slept well."

"I did not."

Dickson's smile slipped. "I am sorry to hear that."

"I'm afraid I haven't slept well since I returned from the peninsula," Colin said as he stepped onto the marbled floor.

"Mr. Burton is in your office," Dickson informed him.

"Excellent," Colin replied. "After I speak to him, I intend to go riding."

Dickson nodded his understanding. "I shall notify the grooms."

"Thank you." Colin proceeded to his study. Entering it, he saw his burly and weathered gamekeeper standing by the window.

"Good morning, Burton," Colin greeted as he walked around his desk.

Burton turned towards him. "Thank you for agreeing to see me," he said.

Colin gestured towards a chair in front of the desk. "Please have a seat."

"I regret to inform you that I have found proof of poaching on your lands," Burton revealed as he sat on the chair.

The gamekeeper had Colin's full attention. "Is that so?"

"I came across a crude trap this morning," Burton shared. "My best guess is that it was intended to catch rabbits."

"That is troubling."

A Tangled Wreath

"That it is," Burton agreed. "We both know poaching is a serious offense and needs to be dealt with swiftly."

"Agreed. What do you intend to do about the problem?"

"I'll go into the village and see if anyone has been selling a large amount of game in the market," Burton said. "Furthermore, with your permission, I shall hire a few men to help me watch the woods."

"That sounds logical."

"With any luck, we will find the person, or persons, responsible for poaching and they will be sent to prison."

"That seems rather harsh for killing some rabbits," Colin mused.

Burton stared at him in astonishment. "For all we know, this person is deer stalking, as well," he said. "If you show any mercy, then it will open you up to even more poachers."

"You are right," Colin conceded. "Have you already informed the constable?"

"I spoke to him before I came to see you."

Colin leaned back in his chair. "Now that that's out of the way, how is your family faring?"

"They are well," Burton replied, puffing his chest out with pride. "My littlest one, Harriet, is going to be ten next month."

"You shall have to wish her a happy birthday from me."

"She will appreciate that."

Colin rose from his chair. "If you will excuse me, it is time for me to get to work," he said. "Good luck to you, Burton."

"Thank you, milord."

After Burton departed from the room, Colin returned to his seat and reached for a ledger. He might as well get some work done before he went riding. He had just reviewed the first page when his mother stepped into the room.

"There you are," she said in an exasperated voice.

"Whatever is the matter?" Colin asked, rising.

"I just received word from Lady Langdon, and she is in desperate need of your help," his mother shared.

"How so?"

"The children from the orphanage in the village are coming to her country home for a Christmas party, and she needs you to select a tree."

"Lady Langdon has more than enough servants who would be up to the task," Colin said, raising his brow. "Why ask me?"

"Because you always manage to find the perfect tree for our manor, and I promised her you would do so for her."

"I'm afraid I am much too busy to be traipsing through the woods to find an elusive tree."

"It isn't elusive. You just have to find the biggest, best looking tree."

"That is quite a tall order."

His mother stopped in front of the desk. "Will you do it?"

"No."

A pout came to her lips. "For the children?" she begged. "It would make them so happy to see such a large tree in Lady Langdon's saloon."

He pursed his lips together, then sighed. "You don't play fair."

"I never have," she joked.

Colin came around his desk and kissed his mother's cheek. "I will go speak to Lady Langdon after my ride."

"Wonderful," she said, clasping her hands together. "I can't wait to see Lady Langdon's expression when you tell her the good news."

Colin eyed her curiously. "What are you about, Mother?"

"Nothing," she replied. "As a patron of the orphanage, I am invested in the success of this party."

Colin didn't believe his mother's suspicious behavior was due to something as simple as that. She was up to something.

Chapter Two

Dressed in her grey riding habit, Arabella departed from her bedchamber and walked down the hall towards her grandmother's room. She stopped in front of the door and knocked, waiting to be invited in.

"Enter," her grandmother called.

Arabella opened the door and stepped inside. "Good morning," she greeted. "How are you faring today?"

Her grandmother reached for a bottle of lotion on her dressing table. "I am well," she replied. "Do you truly intend to go riding this morning?"

"I do."

"Isn't it rather cold to do so?"

"I don't mind riding in the cold," Arabella admitted. "I find it rather refreshing."

Her grandmother started rubbing lotion onto her arms. "Your mother would have said the exact same thing, if she were here," she said. "Nothing deterred Sophie from riding."

Arabella sat on the settee next to the bed. "I miss my mother."

"I know," her grandmother replied. "I miss her, too."

"At times, I can't believe she is truly gone."

Her grandmother smiled tenderly at her. "It will grow easier with the passing of time."

Arabella scoffed. "Apparently, enough time has passed for my father to remarry."

"Try not to be too hard on him," her grandmother advised.

"Why?"

"Because everyone deals with grief in their own way."

Arabella shook her head. "I disagree," she said. "I contend that my father never truly loved my mother in the first place."

"That is rather harsh of you to say."

"I think of her all the time, but I doubt he does."

"Why do you say that?"

"He allowed my stepmother to remove Mother's portrait from the main level and put it in the attic."

Her grandmother frowned. "That might be bad form, but it doesn't mean he doesn't think of your mother."

"If Augusta had her way, she would remove all trace of my mother in our homes, and my father would be complacent," Arabella remarked.

"Your stepmother is still young," her grandmother said. "Most likely, she is intimidated by your mother."

It was Arabella's turn to frown. "You are being entirely too sensible at the moment."

Her grandmother laughed. "I'm afraid that comes with my old age," she responded.

"I just want my life to go back to the way it was before Mother died."

Rising, her grandmother walked over to the settee and sat next to her. "I'm afraid that is impossible," she said. "You must look ahead towards your future."

"My future is bleak."

"Not so," her grandmother contended. "Your future is bright and filled with endless possibilities."

Arabella lifted her brow. "I have had two broken engagements, and my reputation is in tatters," she responded. "I have no doubt that the *ton* will not be kind to me, assuming I even go to Town next Season."

"Where else would you go?"

"I could always remain at our country home for the Season."

"Rubbish," her grandmother declared. "You can't just give up."

"I'm not giving up, but rather choosing to accept my lot in life."

Her grandmother gave her a knowing look. "That sounds a lot like giving up."

"What would you have me do?" Arabella asked, tossing her hands up. "I won't be able to show my face in Town without it being accompanied by gossip."

"You must not give up without a fight."

Arabella's shoulders slumped. "I'm afraid I don't have much of a fight left in me," she admitted. "I am tired."

Her grandmother reached for her hand in her lap. "You have had a rough go of it, but I promise it will get better."

"I am not sure if that is true," Arabella dejectedly replied.

"When I lost my husband, I thought the same way as you are doing now," her grandmother shared. "I thought of him every moment of every day until it nearly consumed me."

"What changed?"

Her grandmother smiled. "I started reflecting on what brought me true joy, and I dwelt on those things."

"Surely it can't be that easy."

"Never underestimate the power of expressing gratitude for the things that we do have," her grandmother advised.

"And that helped you move on after Grandfather died?"

"I have never moved on," her grandmother replied, her tone wistful. "I just learned how to live without him."

Arabella lowered her gaze to her lap. "I doubt I will ever have what you and grandfather had."

"You don't know that."

"I do," Arabella murmured.

Her grandmother released her hand. "Perhaps you need a distraction."

"I could stand to use one."

"The orphans are coming in a few days to decorate a tree in the saloon for Christmas," her grandmother shared. "It would be helpful if you helped select a tree from the woods."

Arabella gave her a baffled look. "Why me?"

"Because I trust you are up to the task."

"I am sure you have many servants who would be able to accomplish the task."

"That may be true, but this party is very important to me," her grandmother said. "I want it to be perfect for the orphans."

Arabella knew that she couldn't refuse her grandmother's simple request, especially since it was for the orphans. "I would be willing to help."

Her grandmother clasped her hands together. "Wonderful," she declared. "The ceilings are high in the saloon, so do not be afraid to select a large tree."

"I think I can manage that."

"I have already made arrangements for someone to assist you," her grandmother said.

Arabella rose. "With any luck, I will find the ideal tree while I am out on my morning ride."

"Do be careful," her grandmother remarked, "and be mindful to stay on our lands."

"That shouldn't be too difficult."

Her grandmother bobbed her head. "Once you return, we can have breakfast in the parlor together."

"That sounds delightful."

"Be on your way, then," her grandmother encouraged.

Arabella leaned forward and kissed her grandmother's cheek. "I shall see you shortly," she said as she stepped back.

A Tangled Wreath

After she departed from the bedchamber, she hurried down the hall and descended the stairs. She was pleased to see that the butler was standing in the entry hall.

Moore smiled as she approached him. "Good morning, milady."

"Good morning," she replied. "I would like to go riding this morning."

"Then I shall see to the arrangements," Moore said, giving her a nod before striding away.

Arabella walked into the drawing room and stared out the window as she waited, admiring the expansive lawn. Was her grandmother right? Should she try to focus on all her blessings rather than her failures?

Arabella sighed. That would be rather difficult; her life seemed to be one mishap after another. How she wished for simpler times!

COLIN LEANED low in the saddle as he raced his horse towards Lady Langdon's manor. Frankly, he didn't mind selecting a tree for Lady Langdon, but he did dread spending any time at her manor. It would bring back a flood of unwelcome memories.

He had spent an enormous amount of time there as a youth and when he was courting Arabella. He had never been as happy as when he was with her, but he'd had a duty to himself and his family. That was not something he could just cast aside or ignore.

It didn't matter now. Arabella was with another, and he hoped she was happy. That is all he had ever wanted for her.

Up ahead, he saw a woman on a horse dart out from the woodlands before disappearing back within. He couldn't help but wonder, who was this brazen person riding on his lands? Well, he was about to find out.

He altered his course, and it wasn't long before he entered the woodlands where he last saw the woman. He slowed his horse's gait and continued down the path until he saw the woman dismounted near a stream.

"You there!" he called as he approached. "What are you doing on my lands?"

The woman turned towards him, and he nearly fell off his horse.

Arabella.

She'd startled at his shout, but quickly recovered. "Good morning, Lord Barrett," she greeted softly.

He lifted his brow at her use of his title, but decided it was best if they had some propriety between them, especially since she was engaged to another. "Good morning, Lady Arabella."

An uncomfortable silence descended over them as he reined in his horse and dismounted, being mindful to maintain proper distance. He took the opportunity to admire her high cheekbones, deep blue eyes, and her pert nose. This is the person he had been dreaming about for five long years, and here she was, standing in front of him.

Arabella laid her hand on her horse's neck. "I do apologize for riding on your lands—"

He interrupted her. "You are always welcome to do so."

"That is kind of you," she replied. "This spot has always brought me such solace."

There was so much to be said between them, but he didn't even know where to begin. Instead, he said, "The weather is beautiful today, is it not?"

"It is," she readily agreed.

He adjusted the reins in his hands as he found strength for his next words. "I am glad we ran into one another. I would like to apologize for how I treated you the last time we were together."

He watched as Arabella visibly tensed. "It matters not."

"It matters to me," he insisted. "I have spent many years

dwelling on it, and I realized how wrong I was to treat you so awfully."

Arabella gave him a curt nod. "I appreciate you saying so."

Her voice lacked warmth, and he knew that she was only appeasing him, so he decided to press her. "But you don't forgive me?"

She grew silent. "The truth of the matter is that you hurt me very deeply, and I have yet to recover from it," she eventually murmured.

He let out a slight huff. "Pardon me if I don't believe you, since you are engaged to another."

Her eyes flashed. "That is none of your concern."

"No?" he asked. "You moved on rather quickly, did you not?"

"If you'll recall, you broke off our engagement, not me," she replied, her voice terse, "and I waited more than four years before I accepted another proposal."

"Good for you," he said dryly. "I hope you will be happy marrying a dandy."

"Lord Eastwood is not a dandy," she countered. "He is just meticulous when it comes to his clothing."

"My apologies, then," he mocked.

Her chin tilted, and she looked away. "Not that it is any of your business, but Lord Eastwood and I are no longer engaged."

"You aren't?" He knew he shouldn't be, but Colin felt elated by the news.

Arabella shook her head. "We each wanted different things."

"Which were?"

"Lord Eastwood wanted to carry on with his mistress, and I wanted a man who would be faithful to me."

"What a scoundrel."

A small smile came to her lips. "I am not going to disagree with that."

"How are you faring?"

All hints of a smile disappeared, and he watched as she pressed her lips together before answering. "I am well."

"Liar," he challenged.

"Why do you say that?"

"Because whenever you lie, you press your lips together first," he revealed. "It has been that way since you were a little girl."

"I had no idea."

"It is just one of the many things that I know about you."

Her eyes grew guarded. "I am not the same girl you knew."

"Is that so?"

Arabella shifted her gaze away from his. "I have had to grow up a lot since you left," she revealed.

"Is that not for the best?"

She met his gaze, her eyes fiery. "You broke off our engagement and left me all alone to deal with the repercussions of it."

"I apologize—"

Arabella put her hand up, stilling his words. "I could handle the stares and whispers, but it was my father's disappointment I was not prepared for. He blamed me for the broken engagement."

He opened his mouth to apologize, but she spoke first. "For the first three years, I was ostracized by the *ton*, but then Lord Eastwood began to show me favor. My life changed for the better, but I had no idea the type of man he was until it was too late."

Colin winced. "For what it is worth, I am truly sorry," he said, hoping his words conveyed his sincerity.

She stared at him for a long moment. "Thank you for that, but what's done is done."

A Tangled Wreath

Feeling compassion swell inside of him, he took a step closer to her, and was devastated to see her step back.

"I should be heading back to my grandmother's," she said. "I wouldn't want her to worry about me."

"That would be wise," Colin replied, but he found that he wasn't quite ready to say goodbye. "Would you like for me to assist you onto your horse?"

"That won't be necessary." She walked her horse over to a fallen tree and used it to mount.

"I had forgotten how independent you are," he joked, hoping to lighten the mood.

Arabella adjusted the skirt of her grey riding habit. "It was good to see you again, even if it was for just a moment."

"Would it be permissible if I called upon you?"

She shook her head. "I don't think that would be a good idea."

"Why not?"

A pained look came to her face. "You made your choice years ago, my lord," she replied.

"I do not like you 'my lord'-ing me," Colin said. "I would prefer it if you called me by my given name."

"It would be entirely inappropriate to do so."

He smiled, hoping to disarm her. "I still intend to call you Bella."

She gave him a scolding look. "You are being entirely too familiar."

"You cannot possibly be in earnest," he said in disbelief. "Whether you like it or not, we have a shared past."

"I am well aware," she responded as she urged her horse forward.

Colin felt his lips curve upward as he watched her ride off. It felt wonderful to see Arabella, but he knew much still needed to be said between them.

Chapter Three

Arabella tried to calm her racing heart as she rode away from Colin. She hadn't been prepared to see him. After five years, there were so many things that she had wanted to say, could have said, but instead she just fled from him.

Coward.

She couldn't seem to find her voice when his mere presence seemed to unsettle her. He had grown even more handsome since the last time she had seen him, and his eyes seemed to bore into her very soul, and she was afraid of what he might see.

She should be incensed at Colin, but her treacherous heart leapt at the sight of him. It was ridiculous! He had broken their engagement and left her to deal with all the gossips without the slightest remorse. No; she would be mindful to avoid Colin from here on out. He wasn't worth her notice, not anymore.

Why hadn't her grandmother warned her that Colin was residing at his country estate? Didn't she realize the animosity Arabella held for him?

Arabella reined in her horse as she approached the stable, effortlessly dismounted, and extended the reins to the groom.

"Did you have a nice ride, milady?" the groom asked.

"I did," she replied. "I intend to go riding later today, as well."

The groom tipped his head. "As you wish."

Arabella slowly walked towards the manor, memories starting to stir deep within her, ones she had tried to forget. The image of her playing on the lawn with Colin came to her mind. They were so young and carefree, and she'd had no idea how he would eventually betray her, taking the last amount of joy she possessed.

Tears came to her eyes, but she blinked them back vehemently. She refused to cry over him now; she had spent entirely too much time dwelling on him over the years. Why couldn't she just banish him from her mind, never think of him again?

She arrived at the main door, which was promptly opened by Moore.

"How was your ride?" he asked, standing aside to allow her entry.

"It was quite pleasant," she lied, stepping into the entry hall. "Is my grandmother in the breakfast parlor?"

Moore shook his head. "No, she is in the drawing room with Lord Barrett, and she has requested that you join them."

Arabella stared at him in disbelief. Why was Colin making a nuisance of himself and showing up unannounced at her grandmother's manor? Furthermore, how had he managed to arrive before she did?

Finding her voice, she asked, "Will you inform my grandmother that I have a headache and that I went to lay down?"

"Yes, milady," Moore said.

Arabella heard Colin's baritone voice wafting out of the drawing room, and she fought the urge to draw closer. She remembered well how his voice had the ability to make her feel things without her ever being touched.

With quick steps, she headed towards the stairs, hoping to

escape unnoticed. She had just put her hand on the iron banister when her grandmother's voice came from behind her.

"Arabella," she said cheerily. "There you are."

She removed her hand and reluctantly turned around. "Here I am," she replied.

"Will you be joining Lord Barrett and I in the drawing room?"

She knew her only recourse would be to lie, so Arabella brought her hand up to her head. "I would, but I have a terrible headache."

"Is that so?"

"It is," she replied. "It is just awful, and I'm afraid I need to go lie down."

Her grandmother gave her a knowing look. "Will you at least come say hello to Lord Barrett?"

Arabella lowered her hand and sighed. She didn't want to admit that she had already spoken to Colin in the woods. "I suppose I could, but only for a moment."

"Wonderful," her grandmother replied.

Dread filled each step as she approached the drawing room. Arabella didn't dare refuse her grandmother's simple request. It wasn't her fault Colin was so insufferable.

He was standing next to the settee and offered her a brief smile when she stepped into the room. He looked dashingly handsome in his blue riding jacket and buff trousers. His hair was brushed forward, and his long sideburns were neatly trimmed.

Arabella had always considered Colin to be the most handsome man she had ever known. He had a square jaw, a straight nose, and eyes that had always entranced her. But his eyes seemed different now. They were filled with a pain that she didn't understand.

Her grandmother stood next to her. "Isn't it wonderful that Lord Barrett has returned home from the war?"

"It is," Arabella answered.

Colin bowed. "It is good to see you looking so well, Lady Arabella."

Arabella dropped into a curtsy, knowing what was expected of her. "You are too kind, my lord."

Her grandmother gestured towards Colin. "Lord Barrett has been gracious enough to volunteer to help you select a tree for this year's Christmas party."

Arabella's heart dropped. She didn't want to spend any time with Colin. Frankly, she didn't trust herself around him. "Surely, he has more important things to do," she attempted.

"Nothing is more important than helping the orphans of this village have a memorable Christmas," he said, challenging her.

"That is most thoughtful, but I have already selected a tree," Arabella lied.

"Did you now?" Colin asked.

She nodded. "It is a glorious tree, and I intend to go mark it so a servant can cut it down."

"I would be more than happy to accompany you," Colin offered.

"That won't be necessary—" Arabella started.

Her grandmother spoke over her. "That would be marvelous."

"Then it is decided," Colin declared, gesturing towards the door with his arm. "Shall we go mark the tree you picked out?"

"Now?"

Colin smiled. "If you are not previously engaged?"

"I'm afraid I have a terrible headache," Arabella said, bringing her hand back up to her forehead. "I would prefer to lie down for a while."

"Of course," Colin responded. "Perhaps I could call upon you this afternoon, after you are properly rested."

"I'm afraid my headache could go well into the night, my lord."

Amusement flickered in Colin's eyes. "I understand, but I do feel as if you shall make a quick recovery."

"Why is that?"

Colin smirked. "I can't help but wonder if your headache was brought on by my presence."

"You wouldn't be wrong," she muttered.

Her grandmother frowned. "Arabella," she chided in a low voice. "Do remember to mind your manners around our guest."

Colin put his hand up. "I do not take offense, especially since I am deserving of Lady Arabella's ire," he said, "but I do hope we can set our differences aside for the sake of the orphans."

"Our differences?" Arabella asked. "Are you referring to how you broke our engagement, thus damaging my reputation in the process?"

He shifted in his stance, having the decency of looking ashamed. "I am."

"Then, my lord," she said dryly, "I can assure you that our differences are indeed too vast to ever hope for a reconciliation."

"I disagree," he replied.

"Regardless, it would be best if we avoided one another while I am staying with my grandmother."

"That would be wise, but what about cutting down the tree for the orphans?" Colin asked. "You wouldn't wish to deny them the simple joy of decorating the tree?"

Arabella pursed her lips together, knowing precisely what he was about. "I have no doubt that you are up to the task."

"Perhaps, but didn't you already select the perfect tree?" he pressed.

Drat. He was using her own words against her, and she had no doubt that he knew she was lying.

"I suppose I can show you where the tree is located."

Colin smiled at her, threatening her resolve to remain

angry at him. "Then I shall call upon you later this afternoon."

"It might be best if we waited until tomorrow."

Her grandmother spoke up. "I would prefer it if we secured the tree today. It would be one less thing for me to worry about."

Knowing she was outnumbered and outplayed, Arabella directed her comments towards Colin. "If that is the case, I shall see you this afternoon."

Colin tipped his head in acknowledgement. "I will be looking forward to it."

Arabella forced a smile to her lips. "As will I."

AFTER COLIN HAD DEPARTED from the drawing room, Arabella turned towards her grandmother with an exasperated look and asked, "How could you invite that audacious man into your home?"

"What would you have me do?" her grandmother asked. "It wasn't as if I could turn him away."

"That is precisely what you should have done."

Her grandmother waved her hand dismissively in front of her. "I wouldn't dream of doing that to him, especially since I have known him since he was born."

"Do you not remember what Lord Barrett did to me?" Arabella asked.

"I do, but—"

Arabella spoke over her. "He broke our engagement and tried to ruin me."

"He did no such thing," her grandmother asserted. "He left because he felt it was his duty to serve in the Royal Army."

"Then why did he offer for me in the first place?"

"I cannot say, but I suspect it was because he had feelings for you."

Arabella huffed. "I thought he did, but I don't believe he could have treated me so despicably if he had."

Her grandmother laid a hand on her sleeve. "You don't know his heart, my dear."

"That may be true, but I know mine," Arabella said. "I was utterly devastated when he abandoned me, especially since I would have waited for him."

"I know, but it is time for you to forgive Colin."

Arabella reared back, surprised by her grandmother's outlandish request. "That is not something I am willing to do."

"You must."

"Why?"

Her grandmother's face softened. "You can't hate him forever."

"I can try," Arabella said. "You seem to forget that I am ruined now and am destined to become a spinster."

"There are worse things."

"Such as?"

"You could have married Lord Eastwood and been miserable for the rest of your days."

"At least I would have had the protection of his name."

Her grandmother dropped her hand to her side. "You don't mean that."

Arabella frowned. "You are right," she admitted, "but I have no prospects now, and my future only looks bleak."

"You just need to be patient," her grandmother encouraged. "Everything will work out exactly the way it is supposed to."

"I'm afraid that is just wishful thinking. Not every person is destined for a happy ending."

"You are still young—"

"I am twenty-two years old."

Her grandmother gave her an amused look. "That is hardly old."

"It is when I am competing with a new crop of debutantes every year."

"I married your grandfather when I was twenty-eight years old," her grandmother revealed.

Arabella lifted her brow. "You were twenty-eight?"

Her grandmother nodded. "My parents were adamant that I would never wed, despite receiving many offers over the years."

"Why did you turn them down?"

"I had no desire to enter into a marriage of convenience."

"But weren't you afraid of becoming a spinster?"

"I was not," her grandmother replied. "I knew what I was looking for in a husband, and I refused to compromise."

"What were you looking for?"

Her grandmother walked over to the settee and sat down. "My father was rather a strict man, but he fiercely loved my mother," she shared. "I knew from a young age that I wanted a love match."

"You were most fortunate to have obtained one."

"It was not without hard work," her grandmother shared. "Henry and I met at a country ball, and for him, it was love at first sight."

"But not for you?"

"Heavens, no," her grandmother replied. "Henry was handsome, but he was entirely too cocky for his own good."

"Is that so?"

"But he was relentless in his pursuit of me," her grandmother said. "He called on me every day until I accepted his offer."

"It sounds as if he wore you down."

Her grandmother smiled. "Sometimes our first impressions are not correct," she remarked. "I was wrong about Henry, and he became the love of my life."

"How I envy you."

"True love will only get you so far," her grandmother

shared. "It is easy to fall in love, but staying in love is an entirely different matter."

"I'm afraid I don't understand."

"The first few months of marriage are utter bliss, but it all changes once you start learning about your spouse's annoying habits."

"Did Grandfather have any annoying habits?"

"Yes, he was a loud chewer," her grandmother revealed. "It would grate on my ears as I ate with him."

"What did you do?"

"It took some time, but I learned to cope with it," her grandmother replied. "You must rise above the small irritants in marriage to enjoy the tender moments that come along with being with the person you love."

Her grandmother continued. "A day does not go by that I don't miss him. He died entirely too young."

"I'm sorry you lost him so long ago."

A wistful smile came to her grandmother's face. "I was blessed to have him in my life for nearly thirty years," she said. "His memory remains with me, and I will always treasure it."

"Not everyone feels as deeply as you do about marriage."

"That is most unfortunate, because anything that is worth doing in this life takes hard work," her grandmother remarked, "and a successful marriage will bring forth great joy."

Arabella shook her head. "Yet my father waited only six months after my mother's death before he wed another."

"I cannot speak for your father's intentions, but he might have been lonely."

"He had me."

"That is not the same thing," her grandmother said.

Arabella pursed her lips together. "I'm afraid I can never forgive him for that."

Her grandmother gave her a knowing look. "Are you

making a list of everyone who has ever wronged you?" she teased.

"That isn't funny. You wouldn't want to forgive them, either."

"When you refuse to forgive, you start to grow resentful," her grandmother said. "That is not the life I want for you."

"The life I had envisioned for myself is gone."

"How do you know that for certain?"

Arabella sighed. "No sensible man will want me now."

"Sometimes the most unsensible men are the most fun," her grandmother joked. "Besides, I intend to leave you an inheritance, so you won't have to want for anything."

"That is most generous of you."

Her grandmother rose from the settee and walked over to her. "You must be patient with yourself and trust that things will work out in your favor."

"I'm afraid patience is not one of my virtues."

"I know, child," her grandmother said. "You have always looked toward the future, but have never learned to enjoy the present."

Arabella winced. "There is some truth to that."

"Only some?"

"You are right," Arabella said. "The last time I truly enjoyed living in the moment was when I was engaged to Colin."

"Why do you suppose that was?"

Arabella stiffened. "It matters not," she declared.

"Of course, it matters—"

"I do not wish to discuss this," Arabella interrupted. "Frankly, there is no point in doing so."

"I just feel—"

"You don't get to have a say about my life." Arabella paused. "I'm sorry, that was terribly unfair of me to say."

Her grandmother's face softened. "You are hurting."

"Quite possibly, but no good will come from dwelling on

this," Arabella said, walking over to the door. "If you will excuse me, I need to go change out of my riding habit."

"You can't keep avoiding talking about this."

"I can try."

Her grandmother gave her a disapproving look, but fortunately didn't press her. "I shall be in the breakfast parlor."

"I'll join you soon," Arabella said as she departed from the room.

Chapter Four

Colin rubbed the scar on his left leg as he sat at his desk in the study. He had been reviewing ledgers for hours and found himself growing increasingly disinterested with each turn of the page.

He had never wanted this life. He had been content serving in the army, fighting alongside his comrades. Now, he spent his days sitting in meetings and discussing farming techniques. There was no adventure, no danger. It was far too predictable for his tastes.

A long clock chimed in the corner, alerting him that it was almost time to call on Arabella. She was a welcome distraction to his boring routine. He could scarcely believe that he saw her this morning. He had dreamed of little else since he had broken their engagement, especially since he had never stopped loving her. How could he? She meant just as much to him now as she did back then. That is why he'd had no choice but to end their engagement, since his paltry income could not provide for her as she deserved.

But his circumstances had changed. He was an earl now, and he had every intention of trying to earn Arabella's affection. He knew that he had hurt her deeply, but would she ever find it in her heart to forgive him?

His brother's voice came from the doorway. "Why do you look so sullen?"

"I'm thinking."

"Does thinking not come naturally to you?"

Colin closed the ledger in front of him and gave his brother an expectant look. "What is it you want, John?" he asked.

John stepped further into the room. "I have come to spend Christmas with you."

"Delightful," Colin muttered.

"According to Mother, you are being insufferable right now," John revealed.

"I daresay she is prone to exaggeration."

"Perhaps, but I found the countryside to be more appealing than staying in Town." John walked over to the drink cart, picked up the decanter, and poured himself a drink. "Luckily for you, the courts are closed until after the holiday."

"Lucky me."

John picked up his glass and walked over to the settee. "Mother was right. You are being rather cranky."

Colin leaned back. "I do apologize. I find reviewing the ledgers puts me in a deplorable mood."

"I am not surprised."

"This," Colin said, waving his hand over his desk, "is not something that I enjoy doing. I gave up a military career to sit behind a desk and attend meetings."

"Most would be envious of your position," John remarked. "You are an earl, and a wealthy one at that."

"Would you be willing to give up being a barrister to help manage the estate?" Colin asked. "I could pay you double what you are earning now."

John took a sip of his drink. "I'm happy where I am."

"That is what I assumed, but I had to at least try."

"If you want me to pity you, I'm afraid you'll be sorely disappointed," John said. "Paul left you a flourishing estate, making you one of the most eligible bachelors in all of England."

"Lovely," Colin grumbled.

"Do you intend to go to London for the Season?"

"I do, but only to take my seat in the House of Lords."

John chuckled. "That's good," he said. "I wouldn't wish for you to enjoy yourself by participating in all the festivities that London offers."

Colin pushed back his chair, rose, and walked over to the window. "I saw Arabella this morning," he revealed a moment later.

John grew solemn. "Is she visiting her grandmother?"

"She is."

"How did it go?" John asked slowly.

Colin frowned. "She hates me."

"Well, I can hardly blame her," John responded. "You broke off your engagement to her."

"For good reason."

"I cannot believe that."

Colin turned around to face his brother. "Arabella deserved better than being tied to me," he explained. "I had no idea when I would return, or if I would return."

John eyed him curiously. "Do you intend to court Arabella now that your circumstances are different?"

"If she will have me."

John rose and walked over to the drink cart. "Are you aware that Arabella was engaged to Lord Eastwood, but he called off the wedding?"

"She informed me of that."

"Did she tell you why?"

Colin shook his head. "She didn't go into specifics."

"Lord Eastwood eloped to Gretna Green with Lady Georgiana," John said. "The rumor amongst the *ton* is that she is increasing."

"Poor Arabella."

"I'm afraid Arabella's reputation will not recover from this," John said. "You may very well be her last hope of ever marrying."

Colin ran a hand through his brown hair. "Arabella has not had an easy go of it, has she?"

"No, she hasn't," John responded. "After you broke off the engagement, she wasn't invited to Almack's, and she was ostracized by some of the families in high Society."

"That must have been devastating for her."

"I imagine it was."

Colin walked over to the drink cart and picked up the decanter. As he poured himself a drink, he said, "When I arrived back in England, I was desolated to discover that Arabella was engaged to another, but I truly thought she was happy."

"Do you believe she is happy now?"

"No, I don't," Colin replied. "I can see sadness lurking in her eyes."

"I can say the same thing about you."

Colin took a sip of his drink. "You don't fight in the army and not pick up a few of your own demons to fight."

"You are home now, and it is time for you to let go of your past."

"I only wish it was that simple," Colin said.

"Why can't it be?"

Colin set his glass down onto the drink cart. "I can't walk long without limping because of my wound."

"That will heal with time."

"It has been nearly eight months."

"You must be patient."

"That is what the doctors keep saying, but I am of a mind that they are all quacks," Colin declared.

John gave him a frustrated look. "Not all doctors are quacks."

"Regardless, I refuse to let the doctor blood-let me again," Colin said. "I hated having leeches on me."

"When did this happen?"

"After I was shot," Colin replied. "I woke up in a tent full of the wounded as the doctor was stitching me up. Afterwards, he suggested I would benefit from bloodletting, and I was too weak to protest."

"I'm sorry that happened to you, but I'm pleased you were able to come home."

"I'm not," Colin replied. "I would have preferred to continue fighting. I was fulfilling my duty to my king and country."

"By taking up your seat in the House of Lords, you are also doing your duty."

"But it is much less exciting."

"I don't dispute that, but earls should not be fighting on the front lines."

Colin picked his drink up again and took a long sip. "I don't know why it matters, since you are my heir."

John put his hands up. "Much like you, I have no desire to be an earl," he protested. "I hope you have a long life and sire many boys."

"If I ever marry."

John smirked. "You will just have to slowly woo Arabella," he said. "You did it once before, and you can do it again."

"The situations were very different," Colin remarked. "I'm afraid it is much more complicated now."

John walked over to the door. "Be careful with her," he counseled. "I have always believed that she was the best thing to ever happen to you."

"I agree."

"Then go convince her of that."

Colin reached out and set his empty glass on the tray. "Wish me luck."

ARABELLA PULLED the needle and thread through the fabric as she glanced over at the window. She had no doubt that Colin would be calling on her soon, but she truly wished he wouldn't. Seeing him again caused a stirring of her old feelings for him. Unwanted feelings; whatever they'd had between them ended the moment he broke off the engagement.

So why couldn't she stop thinking about him?

Regardless, she needed to be mindful of how Colin had mistreated her in the past and protect herself from him. He couldn't be trusted, not anymore.

Her grandmother's voice broke through the silence. "Is everything all right, dear?"

"It is."

"I can't help but notice that you are staring at the window."

Arabella met her grandmother's gaze. "My apologies; I'm afraid I was just woolgathering."

"Were you thinking about anything in particular?"

"Yes, I was thinking about what I shall wear for dinner," she lied.

Her grandmother gave a half shrug. "I just assumed you were thinking about Colin."

"Absolutely not!" Arabella declared. "He isn't worth my notice."

Her grandmother looked amused. "I do believe you protest too much."

Arabella lowered the fabric to her lap. "Colin is an infuriating man whom I do not wish to discuss."

"As you wish."

Silence descended over them as Arabella watched her

grandmother work on her embroidery. Despite her insistent ending of the conversation, she was curious about something, so she asked, "Why did you ask Colin to help select a tree?"

"Because he always picks out the most beautiful trees for his manor."

"If that is the case, why did you ask me to join him?"

Her grandmother set her needlework next to her on the settee. "I thought it would benefit you to spend some time with Colin."

"Why?"

"You two were inseparable growing up," her grandmother said. "It is a shame to throw away a perfectly good friendship."

"It was for a good reason."

"I know, but Colin is home from the war now."

"It doesn't change anything, at least for me."

"It should, especially since he is an earl."

Arabella frowned. "I never cared about acquiring a title," she replied. "I was far more interested in a love match."

"It isn't too late for that."

Before she could reply, Moore stepped into the room and announced, "Lord Barrett is here. Are you available for callers?"

It was on the tip of Arabella's tongue to refuse him when her grandmother spoke up. "Please send him in."

As Moore departed from the room, her grandmother gave her a knowing look. "Ignoring the problem won't make it go away."

Arabella placed her needlework on a side table and smoothed back her blonde hair. She wanted to ensure she looked presentable, and she secretly hoped that Colin still found her attractive.

Colin stepped into the room, wearing a great coat over his clothing. He had a smile on his lips that she found quite aggravating.

After he greeted her grandmother, he met her gaze. "Would you care to show me this divine tree that you have selected?"

Drat. She had lied about selecting the perfect tree.

"I would be happy to," she replied, rising. How hard would it be to find a tree in the woods?

"I assumed we would ride, and the servants would trail behind us in the wagon."

"I am amenable to that plan."

Colin's smile grew. "Shall we?" he asked, offering his arm.

Arabella glanced down at his proffered arm, having no desire to be that close to him. "I assure you that I am more than capable of walking to my own horse unescorted."

"I have no doubt, but it would be my privilege to escort you."

"It would be *your* privilege, but I must refuse your assistance," she said curtly.

Colin withdrew his arm, but his smile remained intact. "Duly noted." He gestured towards the door. "Your horse should be waiting out front."

"Thank you," she replied as she moved past him. She just wanted to pick out this tree and be done with it. The less time she spent with Colin, the better.

Colin came to walk next to her, meeting her stride. "How is your headache?"

"I'm afraid it just started back up again."

He chuckled. "You are a delight, Bella."

Once she'd donned her warm things and they'd mounted their horses, Arabella adjusted the reins in her hand and scanned the woodlands, trying to think of the best place to select a tree.

Colin's amused voice came from next to her. "Where to, my lady?"

She knew he was enjoying her obvious attempt at lying to him. Gesturing towards the woodlands, she said, "This way."

A Tangled Wreath

"Lead on," he encouraged.

Arabella kicked her horse into a run and didn't bother to see if Colin was following her. As they entered the woods, she scanned the trees and tried to find one that would be sufficient for her grandmother's saloon.

Her eyes landed on a pine tree a short distance away. She reined in her horse next to it and announced, "This pine would do nicely."

Colin came to a stop next to her and gave her a skeptical look. "This is your perfect tree?"

"It is," Arabella replied. "What is wrong with it?"

He dismounted his horse and stepped closer to it. "By my estimation, this tree is not even six feet tall."

"It may be small, but it has character," she attempted.

Colin placed his hands on one of the green branches. "The branches are lopsided, and there are gaping holes in the needles."

"That adds to the allure of the tree."

Colin turned back towards her. "You are horrible at picking trees, and I have no choice but to select another."

"I beg your pardon!"

"This tree would frighten the orphans."

Arabella pressed her lips together. "It's not that bad."

"No?"

"It is a perfectly acceptable tree."

Colin crossed his arms over his chest. "The orphans are supposed to decorate the tree for Christmas," he said. "Pray tell, what will they think when they see this pathetic tree in the saloon?"

She tilted her chin stubbornly. "They will admire its character."

"If that is the case, then perhaps we should select two trees for the children to decorate," he suggested.

"I think that is a grand idea."

Colin reached into his pocket and pulled out a red ribbon.

"I will mark this tree for the servants to cut down and we shall proceed to find another tree," he said as he tied the ribbon to a branch.

"Now that I've brought you to the tree I picked, I don't believe my presence is required."

"But it is."

"Why?"

"Because I feel duty-bound to prove to you that I can find a more symmetrical tree in these woodlands."

"I daresay that you would be hard pressed to do so."

Colin stepped closer to her horse and put a hand on its neck. "I could throw a rock and find a better tree than you."

"Prove it, then."

Colin smirked, then he leaned down and picked up a small rock. He threw it towards a cluster of pine trees that were a short distance off. "Shall we see if I was right?"

Arabella cast her eyes back in the direction of the manor, hoping the servants would catch up to them soon. Could she spend additional time with him and pretend that it did not affect her?

Colin's voice broke through her musings. "Bella?"

She brought her gaze back to meet his. "I suppose a few more moments in this cold weather won't hurt."

"It might be best if we walk," he said. "May I assist you off your horse?"

"That won't be necessary." Arabella swiftly dismounted and secured her horse.

Colin watched her with a smile on his face.

"What are you smiling at?"

"You."

"Me?"

He nodded. "You never were one to wait for someone to assist you off your horse."

"Why would I?" she asked, placing a hand on her hip. "I am more than capable of dismounting my own horse."

A Tangled Wreath

"Of course you are," he said. "But that isn't the point."

"Then what is?"

"Never mind," he replied, then pointed towards the pine trees. "It's time I prove to you that I am the master of selecting Christmas trees."

Chapter Five

Colin watched as Arabella walked ahead of him and stifled the groan on his lips. She was keeping him at arm's length, and he wanted nothing more than to break through her defenses; but he knew it would take time.

Arabella stopped and spun around to face him. "Is something wrong?"

"No," he replied. "I was just admiring the lovely weather we are having today."

A brief smile touched her lips. "Are you truly resorting to polite conversational topics to converse with me?"

"I am," he said as he walked towards her.

She gave him a curious look. "Are you limping?"

He stiffened. "I am," he replied curtly. "War injury."

"I assumed as much."

Colin came to a stop in front of her. "If you must know, I was shot in the left leg, and I find myself limping more often than not."

"I am sorry to hear that."

His lips pressed in a tight line. "You don't have to look at me like that."

"How precisely am I looking at you?"

"With pity."

She met his gaze, challenging him. "I'm afraid you are mistaken, my lord," she said firmly. "I see no reason to pity you."

"No?"

"You have all your limbs and your sight, do you not?"

"I do."

"Then you are one of the lucky ones," Arabella replied. "There are many soldiers who fared much worse than you."

"I can agree with that."

"Good," she said. "Now, can we go on with finding this perfect tree of yours before I freeze to death?"

Colin shrugged out of his great coat and draped it over Arabella's shoulders.

"Thank you," she murmured.

They resumed walking towards the cluster of pine trees in silence. Colin tried to think of something to say to her, something that would soften her heart towards him, but he found he was at a loss for words.

Arabella finally broke the silence. "I was sorry to hear about Paul."

"As was I."

"He was much too young to be taken."

"I would agree, but racing boats was his passion."

Arabella tightened the great coat around her. "At least he died doing something he loved."

Colin glanced over at her. "I'm embarrassed to admit that when I first learned about his death, I became angry."

"That's understandable," she said. "Everyone responds to grief differently."

"I'm afraid you misunderstand me. I was angry that he had died, leaving me an earldom."

"Oh," Arabella murmured. "Why was that?"

"I was doing what I loved, but I was forced to come home to take up my seat in the House of Lords."

"Most people would envy you."

"I know I sound ungrateful, but I loved serving in the army," he said. "It gave me a sense of purpose."

He sighed, then continued. "I didn't even get to say goodbye to my comrades," he confessed. "Once my commander received word about my brother, I was sent back on the next ship to England. I was so caught up in the news of Paul's death that I didn't even realize it until later."

"That must have been hard."

"It was, but now…" His voice trailed off for a moment, then he continued, "I feel as if I am adrift."

"Adrift?"

Colin winced. "Quite frankly, I don't know what I want to do with my life," he admitted. "It had been mapped out for me before Paul's death."

"You can do whatever you want now."

"I gave up everything that mattered to me to be in the army," he said, turning his attention towards her. "That is how much I believed in what I was doing."

He could see her visibly tense, but she didn't say anything in response.

Placing a hand on her sleeve, he gently turned her to face him. "Tell me how to make this right between us."

Arabella lowered her gaze to the lapels of his jacket. "I'm afraid it is too late for that," she responded softly.

"Do not say that," he said.

She took a step back. "I should go."

"No," he rushed out. "I still haven't proven my theory about finding the perfect tree."

Colin could see the uncertainty on her face, and he thought she would refuse, but after a moment, to his great relief, she nodded. "All right, but only because I want to prove you wrong."

"I think not," he said, his eyes roaming the ground. "We

first have to find the rock that I threw into the cluster of trees."

"I believe that to be an impossible task."

"I was a scout in the army," he shared. "I have no doubt that I can find a rock."

"You have always been entirely too cocky for your own good," Arabella replied blithely.

"It has served me well." Colin started walking around the spot where he'd seen the rock drop, and in a few moments found it. He leaned down, picked it up, and proudly held it up for her inspection. "I told you that I could find it."

"Thank heavens," she mocked. "I was so worried."

Colin smiled. "You are a minx."

"It is better than being cocky."

"I disagree."

Arabella returned his smile. "I am not surprised."

Colin's eyes dropped to her lips, and he quickly averted his gaze. Clearing his throat, he said, "Now I must find the perfect tree."

"There are many acceptable trees that we could mark."

"I am not looking for an acceptable tree."

"No?"

"I am looking for an extraordinary tree."

Arabella's eyes roamed the area. "I'm afraid that is a lofty goal."

"We shall see," he said as his eyes perused each evergreen. Finally, his eyes landed on one that exceeded his expectations.

Colin walked over to a large pine, which was at least ten feet tall, by his estimation. It was perfect, as if it had been drawn by an artist's hand. The deeply green branches were full and symmetrical.

He held his hand up and proudly announced, "I have succeeded. I have found the perfect tree."

Arabella kept her face expressionless. "It is adequate."

His brow lifted. "Adequate?" he repeated. "I daresay that

A Tangled Wreath

it is more than adequate. This is the finest tree in these woods."

"That is a bold statement," she responded. "Have you seen every tree in these woods?"

He chuckled. "You are just a sore loser."

"I am not."

"This tree is so much better than yours, and you know it." Arabella crossed her arms over her chest. "I suppose we shall let the children decide which one they would prefer to decorate."

"I guess so." Colin removed another red ribbon from his jacket pocket and marked the tree. "We should get you back to the manor now. I wouldn't wish your grandmother to worry about you."

The sound of the servants cutting down the other tree could be heard echoing through the woods.

Colin smirked. "It isn't too late to admit defeat."

"To you? Never."

"I forgot how stubborn you were."

"It is still better than being cocky," she joked.

As much as Colin enjoyed bantering with Arabella, he could see her cheeks had grown pink from the cold air. He knew it was time to get her home and warmed up.

He gestured towards their horses. "Shall we?"

DRESSED in a pink gown with a square neckline, Arabella stopped outside her grandmother's door and knocked.

"Enter," her grandmother said.

Arabella opened the door and stepped into the room. Her grandmother gave her a tender smile from where she stood near her dressing table.

"You look lovely," her grandmother said. "I am pleased that you wore your pink gown, especially this evening."

Arabella gave her a querying look. "Why?"

"Because I invited Lady Barrett and her sons to dine with us," her grandmother revealed.

"Why would you do such a thing?"

Her grandmother lifted her brow. "Do you take issue with Lady Barrett?"

"Of course not," Arabella replied. "I take issue with Colin coming for dinner."

With a dismissive wave of her hand, her grandmother replied, "You will hardly notice his presence."

"I wish you would have asked me before you extended them an invitation."

"Would it have made a difference?" her grandmother asked as she reached for her gloves on the dressing table.

Arabella thought highly of Lady Barrett and John; she simply didn't want to spend the evening with Colin. "I suppose not," she admitted.

Her grandmother nodded in approval. "We shall have such fun this evening!"

"I wish I shared your enthusiasm."

"Chin up, dear," her grandmother encouraged. "You still get along with John, do you not?"

"I do," Arabella responded. "We would occasionally attend the same social gatherings when we were in London."

Her grandmother walked up to her. "Have you considered John as a potential suitor?"

Arabella shook her head. "I think of John like a brother."

"That is a shame," her grandmother replied. "He is a handsome man."

"He may be, but I will always remember the time when he got stung on his bottom by a bee and screamed the entire time he ran home."

Her grandmother laughed. "Poor John! He was only eight." She gestured towards the door. "Shall we go wait for our guests in the drawing room?"

A Tangled Wreath

"I suppose so."

Arabella's eyes roamed over the portraits of her ancestors on the walls as they walked through the house. They landed on a picture of her mother, and she stopped in front of it. Her mother was dressed in a white gown with a purple sash around her waist. Her eyes especially drew Arabella's attention, because they seemed void of any pain, any heartache.

"Your mother was quite beautiful," her grandmother said wistfully.

"That she was."

"I remember when she sat for that portrait. It was the month before she was set to be married to your father."

"Do you think she would be upset at my father's betrayal?"

"I do not think she would view it as a betrayal."

"How could she not?" Arabella asked. "He only waited six months before he married again."

Her grandmother looked over at her. "She would have wanted him to be happy."

"That may be true, but my father should have grieved her properly."

"How do you know he didn't?"

Arabella turned to face her grandmother, and she worked hard to keep the bitterness out of her voice. "I still contend that he never loved her as she loved him."

"That is terribly unfair of you to say," her grandmother said. "You do not know his heart."

"No, but I have seen his actions," she countered, "and they speak volumes."

The sound of knocking at the main door reverberated through the hall, informing them that their guests had arrived.

"You mustn't judge your father too harshly, my dear," her grandmother admonished quietly as they started down the stairs.

"There is not a day that I do not think about my mother,"

Arabella replied. "When I close my eyes, she is the first thing that I see."

"By all appearances, your parents seemed to have a happy union."

"That they did, which is why my father's actions were so unexpected."

Lady Barrett and her sons stepped into the entry hall, stopping any response her grandmother could have given. Arabella noticed that Colin was watching her descent intensely, and she tried to pretend his presence wasn't affecting her. But it was; he'd always had a hold on her, even when they were little.

The moment she stepped down from the last step, Lady Barrett approached her with wide arms and a bright smile. "It is so good to see you, Arabella!" she said as she wrapped her up in a warm embrace.

"Likewise, Lady Barrett," Arabella replied as she leaned back.

She huffed. "You must call me Diane now."

John stepped forward before Arabella could reply and bowed. "It is a delight to see you again," he said. "I believe the last time we spoke was at Lady Linfield's ball."

Arabella nodded. "Yes, you saved me from dancing with Lord Macon, which I appreciated greatly."

"It was my pleasure," John responded.

She turned her attention towards Colin and forced a smile to her lips. "Colin," she greeted.

He tipped his head. "Arabella."

Diane's voice reached her ears, pulling her attention back. "I must see the two trees that you selected after dinner."

"They are both set up in the saloon," Arabella said.

Her grandmother gave her an amused look. "Apparently, Arabella and Colin decided that the orphans needed two trees this year."

A Tangled Wreath

"It is the least that we can do for them," Arabella responded.

"One is rather…interesting," her grandmother teased.

Arabella shrugged. "As I told Colin before, it is full of character."

Colin chuckled. "It looks as if it is half dead."

"That is not true," Arabella defended. "There is plenty of room for the children to decorate the tree."

Moore stepped out into the entry hall and announced dinner was ready.

As they made their way towards the dining room, Colin came to walk next to her. "I was hoping we could go riding tomorrow," he said in a low voice.

"I'm afraid that is an impossibility. I am quite busy tomorrow."

"The day after that, then?"

She frowned. "I'm busy then, as well."

Colin reached for her arm and gently turned her to face him. "Just so you are aware, I am not ready to give up on us."

"I wish you would."

"We were friends once, and I have no doubt that we could be friends once more."

Arabella's eyes darted towards the doorway of the dining room. "This is not the time to be discussing such things."

"Do you not wish to be friends with me?"

She sighed. "It is not that simple, Colin."

"It can be."

Arabella met his gaze. "You can't just try to walk back into my life after five years," she said. "It is terribly unfair of you."

Colin dropped his arm but remained close. "I miss the easy friendship that we once had between us."

"That friendship vanished the moment you broke our engagement," she said sardonically.

"Then I'll work to restore it."

"I should warn you, then, that it would be a waste of your time."

A boyish smile came to his lips, and it threatened to disarm her resolve. "It is my time to waste."

She cocked her head. "Have you always been this infuriating, or is it a recent development?"

Colin chuckled. "I'm afraid you bring it out of me."

"I do no such thing."

He opened his mouth to respond when her grandmother interrupted them. "Will you two be joining us for dinner?" she asked, an amused quirk on her lips.

Colin bowed slightly and gestured towards the door. "After you, my lady."

Chapter Six

Colin sat back and listened to the conversation around him at the dinner table. Frankly, he wasn't in the mood to engage in polite conversation. He was much more interested in finding a way to woo Arabella, but she seemed impervious to his charms. That hadn't always been the case. A smile came to his lips as he thought about how Arabella used to blush around him whenever she was nervous.

His mother's question to Arabella caught his attention. "Did you have a pleasant Season?" she asked.

"It was eventful," Arabella replied vaguely. He noticed that her voice seemed devoid of emotion.

"I was saddened to miss it, but I'm afraid I haven't been in a jovial mood since Paul died," his mother admitted.

"That is understandable," Lady Langdon said. "You must allow yourself a proper amount of time to grieve."

His mother gave Lady Langdon an appreciative smile before asking, "Is there ever enough time to truly grieve a child?"

A silence descended over the table before John spoke up. "I, for one, had an enjoyable Season," he declared.

"I am pleased to hear that," their mother responded.

John reached for his glass. "I was fortunate enough to see Arabella on multiple occasions when we were in Town."

"How joyous," Lady Langdon said.

Arabella smiled. "Besides saving me from dancing with Lord Macon, John was a welcome reprieve from the humdrum of the social gatherings." She smiled. "He is also quite the proficient dancer."

John chuckled. "You flatter me, but we both know that isn't true."

Colin found himself growing increasingly agitated by his brother's interaction with Arabella. It didn't sit well with him that John had danced with her, especially more than once.

"It is true," Arabella pressed. "There are many gentlemen who stepped on my toes, and you weren't one of them."

John took a sip of his drink, then returned the glass to the table. "You never seemed to want for dance partners."

"I wish that were true," Arabella replied.

Lady Langdon wiped the sides of her mouth with her napkin before directing a question to John. "How do you enjoy working as a barrister?"

John's smile remained intact. "I find it to be rather rewarding."

"That is good," Lady Langdon replied.

"I am in a fortunate position where I can help people," John said.

Lady Langdon bobbed her head in approval. "That must be a wonderful feeling."

"As a third son, I knew my options were limited," John responded. "I could either become a vicar or a barrister, and I do not believe the clergy would welcome me into their fold."

"Whyever not?" Lady Langdon asked.

John grinned, unabashed. "I am much too argumentative."

"Then you chose the correct profession," Lady Langdon said.

A Tangled Wreath

"I agree," John responded. "It has served me well these past few years."

Colin leaned to the side as a footman removed the plate in front of him. "You could always have served in the military."

John shook his head. "Again, I am much too argumentative," he said. "I would have been flogged for my impertinence."

"Perhaps, but flogging would have been only one of your concerns," Colin remarked. "You could have been imprisoned in a dark hole or even transported to a disease-ridden colony."

"That sounds awful." John shuddered.

Colin shrugged. "At least you are still alive." He frowned. "I was forced to witness many floggings over the years, some for the most petty offenses."

"I'm sorry you had to endure that," Arabella said quietly.

He met her gaze from across the table. "I had little choice in the matter," he shared. "There were many times I wished I could have commuted the sentence, but it was not my place to do so." He paused. "On one occasion, a soldier died because of his punishment."

"One of our own soldiers was flogged to death?" John murmured, aghast.

"No, not in this circumstance," Colin corrected. "The flogging, though painful, didn't cause his death immediately. His wounds festered, and eventually he died of infection."

"What was the man's crime?" Lady Langdon asked.

Colin hesitated before sharing, "He stole from an officer's tent."

"How terrible," his mother remarked.

With a shake of his head, Colin replied, "What was terrible was that I watched him slowly die right in front of my eyes. He was a robust man before his flogging, but once the infection set in, there was nothing the doctors could do for him. He was forced to endure an agonizing death, and I had no choice but to witness it from a neighboring cot in the medic's tent, unable to move or render any assistance." He paused. "When it is quiet, I can still hear the man's screams as he begged for death."

A dense silence saturated the dining room, and he wondered if he perhaps went too far in sharing his experiences. His pain, his grief, was his own. No one could understand what he had been forced to endure, what he saw in that medic's tent and on the battlefield.

"Well, I am pleased that you are home where you belong," his mother said, breaking the silence. "I constantly worried about you when you were fighting on the peninsula."

"I was doing my duty to king and country," Colin defended.

"That you were," she conceded, "but it is a mother's job to worry."

A footman placed a dessert plate in front of Colin, and he reached for a fork. He was tired of talking about his service in the army. Quite frankly, he should have never brought it up. It always seemed to dampen his mood and it made it difficult to focus on anything else. How could he sit here and engage in menial conversation when the war took so much from him?

Images of his fallen comrades, wounded and dying, came to his mind, and he felt his chest compress. His hands started shaking, the room darkened around him, and the ringing in his ears drowned out all other sound as he fought to breathe. The fork in his hand clattered to the plate with a loud clang, and he startled at the noise, his face flaming in embarrassment.

His mother's voice came from next to him but seemed so far away. "Are you all right, Colin?"

Shoving back his chair, he rose and hurried out of the room. He didn't stop until he arrived at the main door. He threw it open and rushed out. The cold night air penetrated his body, and he put his hands on the back of his head and bent forward as his senses slowly calmed. He couldn't seem to think about his time at war without having a similar reaction. The pain was too raw, too deep.

Arabella's voice broke through the silence. "I came to ensure you were all right."

"You need not concern yourself with me," he said dismissively, though his voice came out a little breathless. He didn't want her to see him in this weakened state.

Unfortunately, she did not take the hint and came to stand next to him. "It is a lovely night, is it not?"

He huffed. "Will you also comment on the state of the gardens?"

"Perhaps," she replied. "I haven't quite decided how this conversation will go."

Colin glanced over and saw that she wasn't wearing a spencer. "You must be freezing," he said. "You should go back inside where it is warm."

"I would prefer to stay out here with you."

"Why?"

"Because I saw your pain. What caused it?"

Colin lowered his hands to his waist. "It is not something I wish to discuss."

"I understand," she replied, but made no attempt to leave.

"Will you not go back inside now?"

Arabella shook her head. "Sometimes a person needs someone to listen to what they aren't saying."

"And what am I not saying?" he asked.

"You may not want to talk about whatever is troubling you, but you don't want to be alone."

He turned to face her. "I am used to being alone."

"That doesn't make it right."

Colin saw the stubborn tilt of her chin and knew that she wouldn't leave him be. He winced before admitting, "I get these images in my head that cause me to grow increasingly agitated. I feel as if I am back in the thick of it, and I can't seem to stop shaking. Once it passes, I feel tired, and I dread another episode."

"There is nothing wrong with admitting that," she said. "Have you spoken to a doctor?"

"I have, but I found his recommendations to be unsatisfactory."

"What were his recommendations?"

"Bloodletting," Colin shared. "He thought the leeches would clean out the toxins in my body."

"Surely, there must be other treatments."

"My old commander had similar episodes, and he used to bathe in cold rivers," Colin said. "He told me that helped him."

"Have you tried smelling lavender to calm you?"

Colin nodded. "Doesn't seem to help."

Arabella placed a hand on his sleeve, providing him with much needed comfort. "You are strong enough to overcome this."

"How can you be sure of that?"

She held his gaze firmly in her own. "Because you are the strongest person I know."

"Not anymore," he murmured.

"I don't believe that to be true, Colin."

He sighed as he shifted his eyes away from hers. He didn't dare admit that he wasn't nearly as strong as he once was only because she was no longer his.

The door opened, and his mother stuck her head out. "We are about to play cards in the drawing room," she revealed. "Would you care to join us?"

Arabella removed her hand and stepped back. "I believe I shall." She gave him a probing look. "Will you be joining us?"

Colin shook his head. "I believe a walk back to my manor is what I need to clear my head."

She gave him a timid smile. "I understand."

After Arabella stepped back inside, Colin started walking

in the direction of his manor. He had a lot to process, and he didn't want to weigh down the others with his pensive mood.

WITH HER HAIR neatly coiffed and dressed in a blue gown, Arabella descended the stairs of the manor and saw Moore was at the bottom to greet her.

"Good morning, milady," the butler said. "I trust that you slept well."

"I did," she replied. "Is my grandmother down yet?"

"She is not, but I expect her shortly."

Arabella's eyes drifted towards the boughs of holly wrapped around the banister and tied with red ribbon. "I see that you have begun to decorate for Christmas."

"That we have," Moore said. "Your grandmother requested that we hang wreaths of evergreen branches from every door on the main level."

"That is quite the feat."

Her grandmother's voice came from behind her. "I want the air to be filled with the scent of pine."

Arabella turned around. "The orphans will be thrilled by the decorations."

"I do hope so," her grandmother said, her eyes lingering on the holly. "This was your grandfather's favorite time of year, as well."

"I hadn't realized."

"He was quite fond of wreaths and insisted they be hung all over the manor."

"Why is that?"

"He often said that our love was like a wreath: never broken, never failing," her grandmother shared.

Arabella smiled. "It warms my heart to know such things."

Her grandmother brought her gaze up, mirth in her eyes.

"He would, however, have criticized that monstrosity that you are trying to pass off as a tree."

"It isn't that bad."

"It is an eyesore. Colin thinks it will frighten the children."

Arabella walked over to the saloon's doors and peered inside. She took only a moment to admire Colin's tree before she turned her attention towards her unique-looking pine. She didn't dare admit that her tree seemed to look even more unfortunate than the last time she had seen it.

"Do you remember when you were afraid of a tree?" her grandmother asked as she came to stand next to her.

Arabella pressed her lips together. "I was eight, and I wasn't afraid of the tree."

"No?" her grandmother asked. "You asked Moore to cut it down."

"That's because that birch tree had long branches that would scrape on my window at night," she said. "It sounded as if someone was trying to enter through the window."

Her grandmother shifted her gaze towards the homely tree. "It isn't too late to have the servants remove this tree and use it for firewood."

"I think the children will appreciate having two trees to decorate."

"Pray tell, why did you and Colin both have to select a tree?"

Arabella stepped back from the door. "Because Colin is entirely too cocky for his own good, and he insulted my choice of tree."

"With good reason," her grandmother teased.

"Colin said that he could throw a rock and pick out a better tree."

"He did succeed on that account."

"*Et tu*, Grandmother?"

Her grandmother laughed. "I will stop making fun of your tree now."

"Thank you," Arabella replied. "Are you ready to go shopping?"

"I am."

They exited the manor and quickly stepped into the awaiting coach. After they were situated, her grandmother rubbed her hands together. "It is rather cold today."

"That it is."

"I should have asked Moore to see to heated bricks."

Arabella reached beneath her and removed a lap robe, which she extended towards her grandmother. "This should keep you warm."

Her grandmother accepted it and settled it over her lap. "Thank you, dear."

As the coach headed towards the village, Arabella kept her gaze on the passing scenery. She chided herself on how she had allowed herself to be unguarded with Colin the previous evening. She needed to be mindful to keep her emotions tucked securely away when she was in his presence.

"You seem deep in thought," her grandmother commented.

"I was just woolgathering."

"About anything in particular?"

She shook her head. "Nothing that you would be interested in."

Thankfully, her grandmother let the matter drop and turned her attention towards the window. "I'm afraid our dear village hasn't changed much since you last visited."

Arabella opened her mouth to respond when the coach jerked to a stop, causing her to fall forward and collide with her grandmother. She put her hands out and assisted her grandmother back onto the bench.

"Are you all right?" she asked.

Her grandmother nodded. "I am."

She heard the driver shouting, so she peered out of the window. To her astonishment, she saw a young boy standing next to the coach, his eyes as round as saucers. He had a dirtied face, mussed-up blond hair, and clothes that did not fit his lanky frame.

Arabella quickly opened the door and stepped out, and the driver stopped shouting at the boy.

"I do apologize, milady," the driver said, "but this urchin ran out in the middle of the street."

"I understand, but I think he has been given a thorough tongue lashing." She turned her attention towards the boy. "Are you hurt?"

He shook his head hesitantly but didn't speak.

"The lady asked you a question, boy!" the driver shouted from his perch.

Arabella turned towards the man. "Thank you for your assistance, but I shall handle this on my own."

The driver tipped his head in response.

She returned her attention towards the boy. "How old are you?"

The boy stared at her, a bewildered look on his face.

"Can you not speak?" she asked.

"I can speak," the boy replied shakily. "I am twelve years old."

"What is your name?"

"Peter."

She leaned closer to him and smiled. "It is nice to meet you, Peter," she said. "My name is Arabella."

Peter lowered his gaze towards the ground. "Hello."

"May I ask why you were in the street?" she asked.

"I had to get to the other side."

"I can't fault that logic."

The smell of freshly made bread wafted in the air and she saw Peter rub a hand over his stomach. She reached into her reticle and said, "I have an errand that I need you to run."

Peter looked up at her in surprise. "Me?"

She removed two coins and extended them towards him.

"I would like you to purchase some bread and deliver it to me at the milliner's shop," she said. "Do you know where that is?"

"I do," he responded, accepting the coins.

"One coin should pay for the bread and the other is for your time," she explained.

The boy clutched the coins in his hand. "I will be right back."

"See that you are," she replied.

Arabella watched as the boy ran off and heard her grandmother's voice from the coach. "I fear that your trust may be misplaced."

"Perhaps, but I hope he uses that money to purchase himself some food."

She stepped into the coach, and they rode the short distance to the milliner shop. As she exited the coach, she saw Peter running up to her with a loaf of bread in his hand.

He came to a stop in front of her, his breathing labored. "I got yer bread," he said, holding it up.

"I'm afraid I am not very hungry anymore," she said. "By chance, are you hungry?"

Peter nodded vehemently. "I am."

"I am glad to hear that," she responded. "Will you be kind enough to eat that for me?"

The boy smiled widely. "I will." He ran a short distance away, stopped and spun back around. "Thank you, miss!"

Arabella felt a smile growing on her lips as she watched the boy's retreating figure. It felt good to help someone, even though she knew her contribution was minimal.

Her grandmother came to stand next to her. "It would appear that you brightened his day."

"I hope so."

"We better get inside before we freeze to death," her grandmother encouraged.

Dear Margarette

Langdon Hall, Maidstone
December 21, 1815

I wish you were here at Langdon Hall, because you would not believe the great lengths that Arabella is taking to avoid Colin! It would be amusing if she weren't hurting so. She is still quite upset about him breaking their betrothal before leaving for war, and I fear it is clouding her judgement.

Since we are not spending Christmas together, I decided it would be the perfect opportunity to invite the orphans in the village to come decorate the tree in the saloon and sing songs on Christmas Eve. I asked Arabella to select a tree with Colin, but they ended up arguing most of the time and selected two trees. Two! Can you imagine? Furthermore, the one Arabella selected is peculiar and looks awful next to the grand one Colin procured. I have no doubt that she selected it out of haste just to be rid of him.

It is evident to everyone that Colin is not the same man he was five years ago. Well, evident to everyone but Arabella. She still sees him as only the man who broke her heart. Colin's mother, Lady Barrett, says that her son has changed since seeing Arabella again. He isn't nearly as boorish, which is something Lady Barrett thought impossible.

This is my first attempt at matchmaking, and I fear that I am awful at it. I must find a way to push Colin and Arabella together without inadvertently pushing them apart. It is proving to be a much more difficult task than I ever imagined.

I am sending well wishes to you and your matchmaking attempt. I hope you are not encountering any problems.

Fondly yours,
Esther

Chapter Seven

Colin raised his pistol and fired, hitting the middle of the target. Then he handed it off to the footman so he could reload.

John's voice came from behind him. "Well done."

Colin turned to face his brother. "Would you care to try?"

John put his hands up. "I do not dare, as I know I would make a fool of myself."

"Surely, you cannot be that bad."

John chuckled. "I assure you that I am."

"I have discovered that shooting pistols relaxes me."

"That is odd, brother."

The footman handed the pistol back and Colin accepted it. He turned around, aimed at the target, and fired. He was pleased to see it hit dead center again.

"You have been shooting for hours," John commented. "Is everything all right?"

"It will be."

"Mother is worried about you."

"She has no reason to be."

John came to stand next to him. "You have hardly said a word to anyone since last night."

"I am talking to you now," Colin pointed out.

"That you are, but you haven't explained why you left the dinner party and walked home."

"I didn't realize I answered to you," Colin remarked dryly.

"You don't, but we are concerned about you."

Colin extended the pistol towards the footman as he said, "Let me save you some breath; I am fine."

"Are you?"

"I am."

John frowned. "Then pray tell, why did you leave the dinner party last night?"

"Didn't Arabella explain my absence?"

"She only said that you needed some time to think. I'm glad she had the foresight to send a footman after you with your coat."

Colin nodded in approval. "She wasn't wrong."

"What did you need to think about?" John asked.

"Why is it so important for you to know?"

"Because we are family."

"That we are, but sometimes it is best to leave things unsaid."

John walked over to the footman and held his hand out for the pistol. He weighed it in his hand for a few moments before he brought it up. The pistol discharged, and the bullet hit the outer ring of the target.

"Impressive shot," Colin praised.

John grinned. "We both know that isn't true."

"You hit the target."

"I did, but you managed to hit the center every time."

"That is because my aim was the difference between life or death for me."

John gave the pistol to the footman. "You must have seen some terrible things while you were fighting in the war."

Colin's jaw clenched. "I did."

"I couldn't help but notice your demeanor changed last

night when we were talking about the army, as it has right now."

"I do not like discussing the war."

John's gaze left his to roam over the east lawn. "I can't even pretend to imagine what you must have endured over there, but you are home now."

"Not by choice."

"What do you mean by that?"

"I was ordered to come home because of Paul's death," Colin explained. "If it were up to me, I would still be in the Army."

"I see."

"Do you?" Colin asked, his voice rising. "Because I feel as if I abandoned my fellow soldiers."

John gave him a sympathetic look. "You did no such thing," he said. "Besides, you were injured."

"Everyone was injured, in one way or another."

"It is time for you to start healing."

Colin shook his head. "I'm afraid that is impossible."

"Why?"

"I have seen too many horrible things to ever think I could go back to how I once was," Colin said. "Quite frankly, I have done terrible things in the name of the Crown."

"You were duty-bound."

"I was, but it still taxes the soul."

John took a step closer to him. "You have done your part in the war, but your mind still seems far away. It is time for all of you to come home."

"You don't know what you are asking of me," Colin said.

"I know precisely what I am asking of you."

Colin shifted his gaze away from his brother. "I should have been killed, but I survived when others did not."

"It is not uncommon for soldiers to feel this way."

Colin turned towards the footmen and abruptly ordered, "Leave us."

Once they were alone, Colin faced his brother. "What I'm about to share must remain between us."

John grew serious. "I understand."

Colin hesitated before he started speaking, his words coming out slowly. "It was my third assignment, and I was partnered with Sam Burkard. We were ordered to sneak into the enemy camp and search the officers' tents for documents that might aid in the war."

"That seems rather dangerous."

"You take risks when you are at war," Colin said. "Sam and I succeeded in finding documents that informed us of troop placement, but we weren't so lucky when we departed from the tent."

"What happened?"

"A guard saw us and sounded the alarm."

"How did you escape?"

Colin pursed his lips together. "Sam shoved the documents in my hands and told me to run," he shared.

"And did you?"

"I tried to argue with him, but he was adamant," Colin said. "He told me that I was the fastest runner, and I had a better chance of escaping to deliver the documents." He hesitated. "When I heard the French soldiers approaching, I turned and ran deeper into the woods."

John watched him closely, but didn't say anything.

"I went back to our camp, and I waited all night for Sam to come home. But he never did." Colin sighed. "The next morning, I went in search of him, and I found his body hanging from a tree near where I left him."

"I'm sorry to hear that."

"I was praised for my heroics by my commanders, since those documents helped turn the tide of the war," Colin said. "But it was Sam who was the true hero."

John stepped closer and set a hand on his shoulder. "You did nothing wrong."

A Tangled Wreath

"I did. I left Sam."

"If you had stayed, you would have been killed, as well."

"We could have fought them off together," Colin attempted.

John lifted his brow. "I doubt you could have fought off an entire camp of French soldiers," he said. "Furthermore, you had information in your possession that aided in the war."

"It doesn't take away the image of his lifeless body."

"No, I suppose it does not," John admitted, removing his arm.

Colin winced. "I've tried to find his family, but I haven't been able to locate them."

"For what purpose?"

"I don't know their situation, but I want to ensure they are always taken care of."

"That is most thoughtful of you."

"It is the least I can do for the man who gave his life for mine."

John tipped his head. "I can use my contacts to look into the location of Sam Burkard's family, as well."

"That would be most appreciated…" His words trailed off as he saw Arabella ride her horse towards the woodlands.

John followed his gaze. "Go on, then," he encouraged.

"I'm only going to speak to her because I am worried about her," Colin said, backing up. "After all, there are poachers in the woods."

John didn't look convinced. "If that is the only reason…" He left his sentence dangling, a knowing smile on his lips.

"It is."

ARABELLA STOOD next to the stream and listened to the soothing sound of the water trickling over the rocks. Her thoughts turned to her mother, and she was reminded that this would be her first Christmas without her.

How Arabella missed her. She missed her strength, her kindness, and her ability to make everything feel all right, even when everything seemed to be crashing down around her. Her mother was a formidable woman who had taught her so much over the years. How was she supposed to go on without her?

She reached up to wipe away the tears in her eyes. She had cried so much over her mother these past six months, but it didn't seem to ease her pain. Nothing seemed to help the gnawing ache deep within her.

Arabella turned her head at the sound of a rider's approach. She was surprised to see Colin watching her intently from atop his horse.

He reined in near her. "I came to warn you that there are poachers in these woods."

She turned away from him so he wouldn't see her tear-stained face. "Thank you for your concern," she replied. "I shall use caution, then."

Colin didn't say anything for a long moment. "You have been crying," he finally said.

"I have," she replied, seeing no reason to deny it.

"Are you all right?"

Arabella met his gaze. "I was just thinking about my mother."

"I was saddened to hear about her passing," Colin said. "She was a remarkable woman."

"She was."

Colin dismounted his horse and secured it. "I received word that she had passed, but I didn't hear any particulars."

"I'm afraid it was rather sudden. She collapsed and never regained consciousness," Arabella informed him. "The doctor said her heart failed her."

"I am sorry to hear that."

"Thank you," she replied. "I'm afraid I didn't even have a chance to say goodbye."

"That must have been hard."

Arabella nodded. "I always considered my mother to be the strongest woman I know. I never thought she would die at such a young age."

"Death is no respecter of persons."

"No, it is not." Arabella paused. "I apologize for going on. I know that you have had your share of death, as well."

"You never have to apologize to me, especially when you are speaking from the heart," Colin said.

"That is kind of you to say."

"There is nothing kind about it," he replied, his eyes growing intense. "You may not consider me a friend, but I think of you as one."

Arabella's horse whinnied, drawing her attention. "I should go."

"Must you?" Colin asked.

She wasn't quite ready to say goodbye to Colin, but she didn't dare admit that. She knew she was being reckless with her heart by even spending this moment in his presence. However, it felt like a reprieve to talk to him. His voice had always been able to soothe her troubled soul.

She came to a decision, despite her misgivings. "I suppose I could tarry for a little longer." They stared at one another, and before it grew awkward, she asked, "How are you enjoying managing the estate?"

Colin let out a groan. "It is awful."

"Why do you say that?"

"I spend the majority of the day in meetings," Colin said. "Furthermore, I have debated about throwing the ledgers out of the window on more than one occasion."

"Surely, it can't be that bad?" she questioned.

"It's worse," he replied. "This was not a life that I ever wanted."

"I know, but you are in a position to enact real change."

Colin ran a hand through his hair. "I'm afraid I do not care about farming techniques," he admitted. "I would much rather be doing something worthwhile."

"That is terribly unfair of you to say," she chided. "You are responsible for many people and their livelihoods."

"I know I sound ungrateful, but I do not want to spend the remainder of my days sitting behind a desk."

"Then don't."

Colin cocked his head. "Pardon?"

Arabella took a step closer to him. "You can forge your own path."

"And the ledgers?"

"I didn't say you wouldn't have to do some work, but you can spend your time amongst your tenants."

"For what purpose?"

"Do you even know your tenants?" she asked.

He shook his head. "I own too much land to know all of my tenants."

"You should change that."

"That is why I employ a steward."

"Have you attempted to get to know any of them?"

"I attend the meetings, and I have listened to their many complaints," Colin responded. "It is exhausting to hear about all that needs to be tended to."

Arabella gave him a knowing look. "Why did you join the Royal Army?"

"That's simple," he replied. "I wanted to fight for my country."

She put her hands out and asked, "You fought for this, did you not?"

"It's not that simple."

"I do not wish to presume to know the great responsibility that you have been given, but I envy you."

Colin looked at her curiously. "Envy me? Why?"

"You have the freedom to do as you please."

"And you don't?"

Arabella shook her head. "My options are limited, I'm afraid," she sighed. "I am sad to admit that my future looks rather bleak."

"I don't believe that to be true."

Arabella shifted her gaze away from his. "My own father doesn't want me around."

"He said that to you?"

"No, but he sent me away for Christmas," she said dejectedly. "He wanted to spend the holiday with his new wife."

"That doesn't sound like the man I knew growing up."

Arabella walked over to a fallen tree and sat down. "He changed after my mother died," she responded. "I feel as if I have lost both of my parents."

"Grief can change people."

"Perhaps, but his new wife is just awful," Arabella said. "She is my nemesis."

"You have a nemesis?" Colin lifted his brow, amusement in his voice.

"I do," she replied. "Augusta does everything in her power to drive a wedge between my father and I."

"If I recall correctly, isn't she rather young?"

Arabella bobbed her head. "She is only five years older than me," she responded. "I know my father only married her so he could get the precious heir that he always wanted."

"He wouldn't be the first man to do so."

"No, but that is one of the reasons why I accepted Lord Eastwood's offer," she admitted. "I felt like an interloper in my own home, and I knew I needed to establish my own household."

"What were the other reasons?"

Arabella pursed her lips, delaying her response. "My reasons are my own."

"I respect that, but I am trying to make sense of why you ever agreed to marry that lout in the first place."

"He was very handsome."

"More so than me?"

Arabella closed her eyes, knowing that Colin was intentionally goading her. "I never said that," she murmured.

Colin took a step closer to her. "Why did you accept Lord Eastwood's offer of marriage?" he asked softly.

She brought her gaze up as she boldly admitted, "I knew I could never fall in love with him."

Surprise registered on Colin's face. "I'm afraid I don't understand," he said. "Why would you want a loveless marriage?"

"Because it is much easier that way."

"How so?"

Arabella took a step back, creating more distance between them. "I couldn't risk losing my heart again."

He winced. "That doesn't sound like you, Bella."

"I'm afraid I was forced to grow up after you left me, and I realized that love was a trivial emotion."

"It isn't trivial."

"No?" Arabella asked. "Pardon me if I don't believe you. You spoke of love to me once, but you walked away from it."

Colin opened his mouth to reply but she spoke first. "It would be best if I departed."

"Bella..."

"Please don't say anything," she said. "I shouldn't have brought it up. It wasn't fair of me to do so."

"We need to discuss this."

Walking over to her horse, she used a fallen log to assist her onto the side saddle. "I would prefer not to."

"May I ask why?"

"Because you lost that right when you broke our engagement."

He approached her horse and put a hand on the gelding's

neck. "I would like to explain my reasons for doing so," he pleaded.

"I'm sorry, but I am not interested."

Arabella urged her horse forward, ignoring the crestfallen look on Colin's face. She knew she was being entirely unfair to him, but she needed to protect her heart.

Chapter Eight

Colin stared out the window at the mist that hung low in the gardens as the morning sun streamed into his bedchamber. He'd had the most fitful night of sleep, and it was all because of Arabella. There were so many things he wanted to say to her, that he needed to say. It wasn't just because he wanted to clear his conscience; he wanted her to know the truth.

But she'd refused to listen.

Not that he blamed her. He had treated her terribly, and she had every right to hate him. At times he could see her softening towards him, but then she'd blink, and her eyes would become guarded. How could he make her understand that he broke the engagement for her own good?

His valet's voice came from behind him. "Which cravat would you care to wear today?"

"I care not," Colin grumbled. "Just give me a blasted cravat."

"White, it is."

Colin turned around to face the man. "Why is it that it is easier to fight in a war than it is to converse with a lady?"

"It usually is." Simon gave him a knowing look. "I must assume that you are speaking of Lady Arabella."

"I am."

Simon approached with the cravat. "Women are finical creatures, and you must approach them as you would a skittish horse."

"I would agree, but Arabella is so..." His voice trailed off as he attempted to find the word that would describe her. "Complicated."

"That does describe most women, my lord."

Colin finally accepted the cravat and started tying it around his neck. "It was much easier when we were on the peninsula."

"That may be true, but I must admit I prefer sleeping on a bed than the ground."

"As do I," Colin agreed as he dropped his hands.

Simon extended him a blue jacket. "I would encourage you to be patient with Lady Arabella," he said. "You aren't trying to win a battle, but the war."

"You make a good point."

"I usually do," Simon replied, smiling.

Colin chuckled as he walked over to the door. "I shall see you after my ride."

Colin found his mother standing at the top of the stairs, speaking to a maid. He waited politely for her to finish before he leaned in and kissed her cheek. "Mother," he greeted. "How are you this morning?"

"I am well," she replied.

"Do you intend to join us for breakfast this morning?"

She nodded. "I do."

"Wonderful," he replied, offering his arm. "Allow me the privilege of escorting you to the dining room."

As she placed her hand on his sleeve, she said, "I'm afraid I haven't seen very much of you these past few days."

"That isn't true," he responded. "We saw each other when we dined with Lady Langdon."

"But you left early," she pointed out.

"I did."

"With no real explanation."

Colin glanced over at her. "I believe you already had John interrogate me."

"I did, but it didn't yield the results I was hoping for."

"Meaning?"

His mother stopped on the bottom step and turned to face him. "John didn't really tell me anything useful."

"Why do you suppose that was?"

"Either he is protecting you, or you haven't confided in him." She paused. "I suspect it is the former."

"What would he need to protect me from?"

His mother eyed him with concern. "Yourself."

Colin rested his hands on his mother's shoulders and leaned in. "I am fine, Mother."

"Are you?"

"I am."

A frown came to her lips. "I am worried about you."

"I know, and I love you even more because of it."

"You will come to me if you need help, won't you?"

Dropping his arms to his sides, Colin replied, "I can promise that."

His brother's voice came from the top of the stairs. "Was I not notified of a family meeting?" John joked as he descended the stairs.

"Colin was just reassuring me that all is well with him," his mother shared.

John grinned. "What a relief." He came to a stop next to them. "Is anyone else famished, or is this meeting not over?"

As they walked towards the dining room, their mother said, "I have been thinking we should have Lady Langdon and Lady Arabella over for Christmas Eve dinner."

"That would be most thoughtful," John remarked.

"It would." She turned her gaze towards her other son. "What are your thoughts on the matter, Colin?"

"I am not opposed to dining with them."

His mother nodded approvingly. "I'll need to send the invitation straight away, but I'm afraid I do not have a servant to spare to deliver it."

Colin lifted his brow. "I find that rather farfetched."

"It is true," she replied with a wave of her hand. "They are all busy decorating the manor for Christmas."

"All of them?" he questioned in disbelief.

She bobbed her head. "Yes, every single one of them."

"But we have over a hundred servants who work here."

"I am well aware, but don't you want the decorations to be perfect?"

Colin gave her an exasperated look. "I am confident that you can spare one servant for an errand."

"I'm afraid that is an impossibility."

He stopped outside the dining room and allowed his mother to enter first. John came to stand next to him and lowered his voice. "You do realize that Mother won't stop until you agree to deliver the invitation yourself?"

"I do."

"I'm glad to hear it," John responded as he patted him on the shoulder.

Colin stepped into the dining room and said, "If all of the servants are busy, I would be happy to deliver the invitation to Lady Langdon."

His mother smiled brightly. "That is most thoughtful of you, but are you sure it won't be too much of a bother?" she asked innocently.

"I am sure," he said, stepping up to the buffet.

After he filled his plate with food, Colin sat at the head of the table. His mother was seated to the right of him, sipping her tea.

John sat down next to him. "Do you intend to go riding today?"

"I do."

A Tangled Wreath

"Would you care for some company?"

Colin nodded. "I would," he replied. "Shall we plan to go riding after I return from delivering the invitation to Lady Langdon?"

"I will be waiting."

His mother reached into the pocket of her lavender gown and removed a folded piece of paper. "Fortunately, I took the liberty of already writing it out," she said, extending it to him.

He accepted the note. "Why am I not surprised by this?"

"I correctly assumed that you would have no objections to inviting them to dinner," his mother remarked.

Colin slipped the note into the jacket of his pocket. "I shall see to it."

"Thank you," his mother said. "Please inform them that we will light the Yule Log as part of our Christmas Eve celebration."

"That is a silly tradition," Colin muttered.

"It is not," his mother defended.

John wiped the sides of his mouth with his napkin. "I refuse to sit upon the log before it goes into the fireplace."

Colin interjected, "I am of the same mind as John."

"But it is deemed good luck," his mother attempted.

"I shall take my chances," John responded.

Their mother gave them a disapproving look. "Regardless, we shall light the log from a lump of charcoal left over from last year's Yule Log."

"I take no issue with that," Colin said, reaching for his fork, "especially since I know how much you value traditions."

His mother gave him a sad smile. "Your father used to be the one that lit the Yule Log every year," she shared. "It was that way since we were married."

"Who lit the Yule Log last year?" Colin asked.

His mother grew quiet. "Paul."

Colin set his fork down and slipped his hand over his mother's. "Did Paul sit on the log?"

"He did," his mother replied.

Colin exchanged a look with John before saying, "Then we shall all sit on the log."

"Thank you," his mother murmured. "I am sorry that my emotions are getting the best of me."

"You have no reason to apologize," Colin rushed to assure her. "The wounds are still raw for all of us."

His mother abruptly rose. "I'm afraid I will need a moment to collect myself."

Colin rose and watched as his mother swiftly walked out of the room.

John spoke up. "At times, I hear her crying in her bedchamber."

"I wish there was a way to help her."

"She lost both her husband and her son in a short period of time," John said. "She just needs time to grieve properly."

Colin stared at the empty doorway, knowing there were some things he couldn't fix. And that greatly bothered him.

ARABELLA PULLED the thread through the needle's eye as she sat across from her grandmother. They had been working on needlework for the past hour, and she was growing dreadfully bored. Perhaps it was time to adjourn to the library and select a book to read.

Her grandmother must have noticed her restlessness. "Whatever is the matter?" she asked.

"I'm bored."

Her grandmother chuckled. "I'm afraid I can't help you with that, dear."

Arabella glanced over at the window. "Would you care to go on a walk through the gardens?"

"It is entirely too cold for me."

"We could go shopping."

A Tangled Wreath

Her grandmother lowered her needlework to her lap. "We visited the shops yesterday."

"I could read to you," Arabella suggested.

"If you did, I'm afraid I would just fall asleep."

"There is no shame in that."

Moore stepped into the room with a tray in his hand. "A letter has been delivered for Lady Arabella."

She perked up. "Is that so?"

Moore approached her and extended the tray. "It is from a Lord Eastwood."

Arabella's heart dropped as she reached for the letter. "Did you say Lord Eastwood?" she asked.

"I did," Moore replied, looking unsure.

She glanced down at the letter in her hand and considered tossing it into the hearth. He had no business writing to her, not since he had broken their engagement.

Her grandmother spoke up. "Are you going to read it?"

"I'm not sure."

"Would you care for me to read it?"

Arabella shook her head. "That won't be necessary," she said as she unfolded the paper. "I will read it, but only because I find myself most curious."

As she read the contents of the letter, she found herself growing increasingly irritated by Lord Eastwood's pretentious attitude.

"He has some nerve!" she exclaimed, crumbling the paper in her hand.

Her grandmother gave her an expectant look. "Whatever did he say?"

"Lord Eastwood apologized for eloping with Lady Georgiana, and begged for my forgiveness," Arabella explained.

"It was an apology letter?"

"No," Arabella replied with a shake of her head. "Lord Eastwood's father caught up to them before they were married and forbid him from marrying Lady Georgiana."

"So what did Lord Eastwood do?"

"He left her in Gretna Green and traveled back with his father," Arabella said.

Her grandmother gasped. "How horrible!"

"Now Lord Eastwood is hoping that we can post the banns and 'put this unfortunate incident behind us'."

"He still wants to marry you?"

"Apparently so."

"What say you?"

Arabella huffed. "I wouldn't marry him if he were the last man in Town."

"I must admit that I am relieved to hear that," her grandmother said.

Rising, Arabella walked over to the window and stared out. "I may have been foolish enough once to accept his offer, but I refuse to do so again."

"Lord Eastwood is a..." her grandmother lowered her voice, "scoundrel."

"That he is," Arabella agreed. "I didn't think I could feel sympathy for Lady Georgiana, but I was wrong. He treated her most distastefully."

"That he did," her grandmother agreed. "She is ruined."

Arabella grinned. "Perhaps we could live together as spinsters," she joked.

"Your situations are entirely different."

"That may be true, but I still have two broken engagements," Arabella said.

"You are just waiting for the right man."

Arabella turned around to face her grandmother. "I'm not sure if that is true anymore."

"You mustn't give up hope."

"It's hard not to," Arabella admitted.

Moore stepped into the room once more and announced, "Lord Barrett has requested a moment of your time."

Her grandmother nodded. "Please send him in."

Arabella turned back towards the window, trying to ignore her racing heart. Why had the thought of seeing Colin caused her to react in such a way? It was very inconvenient.

Colin's voice came from the doorway. "Thank you for agreeing to see me," he said, stepping further into the room.

"Would you care for some tea?" her grandmother asked.

"I would," he replied. She procured and poured a cup for him, which he accepted. "Thank you."

Her grandmother leaned back in her seat and asked, "How may we help you today?"

He took a sip of his tea before setting it down on the table. "My mother asked me to deliver this invitation to you," he responded as he retrieved a folded piece of paper from his jacket pocket.

"That is most thoughtful of you," her grandmother said.

Arabella turned towards him. "Was it truly necessary for you to personally deliver the invitation?"

Colin smirked. "It would appear that all of the servants are rather busy at my estate."

"All of your servants?" she repeated back in disbelief.

"So I was told by my mother." He handed the invitation to her grandmother. "We are hoping you will join us for Christmas Eve dinner."

Her grandmother smiled brightly. "What fun we shall have!"

Colin nodded. "My mother will be pleased that you will be joining us." He lifted his brow. "Assuming that is acceptable to you, Bella."

Arabella forced a smile. "It sounds like it will be a memorable evening."

Colin gave her an odd look. "May I speak to you for a moment?"

"Is that truly necessary?" she asked.

"I assure you that it is."

She sighed. "We can take a tour around the garden," she

acquiesced, turning her gaze toward her grandmother. "Do we have permission to do so?"

"Of course," her grandmother replied.

They made their way outside and started walking down the path, Arabella's hands firmly clasped in front of her.

Colin glanced over at her. "Do you want to explain why you are upset?"

"I am not upset."

"No?" he asked. "Then why do I see pain in your eyes?"

"I know not," she said, lowering her gaze.

He stopped and put a hand on her sleeve, turning her to face him. "It's me, Bella," he said softly. "What's wrong?"

Unbidden tears came to her eyes, and she attempted to blink them back. The kindness in his voice was her undoing, and she found herself revealing, "Lord Eastwood has offered for me again."

"When was this?"

"I received the letter only moments before you arrived."

Colin ran a hand through his hair. "I thought he eloped with Lady Georgiana to Gretna Green?"

"He did, but his father stopped the wedding."

"I see." He grew silent. "Do you want to marry him?"

Arabella shook her head, the curls that framed her face swaying back and forth. "I do not."

"Then why are you upset?"

"Lord Eastwood wrote in the letter that he had my father's blessing for us to wed," Arabella admitted, bringing her gaze up.

"Why does that upset you?"

"Even though Lord Eastwood treated me most terribly, my father still gave his permission for us to wed," Arabella said. "I daresay that I am just a burden to him."

"That cannot possibly be true," Colin asserted. "You are not a burden to anyone."

Arabella shifted her gaze away from his. "What if my

A Tangled Wreath

father disowns me if I don't marry Lord Eastwood?"

"Has he given you any indication that he would do something so cruel and unfeeling?"

"No, but I hardly recognize the man that he has become without my mother."

Colin stepped closer to her and placed his hands on her shoulders. "You don't need to worry about your future."

She reached up and wiped the tear that was rolling down her cheek. "That is easy for you to say."

"It's true," he said. "I promise you that you will never lack for anything."

"You can't promise me that," she said. "At least, not anymore."

"Why?"

Arabella took a step back, causing his arms to drop. "If you truly meant that then we would have already been wed."

"Bella—"

She put her hand up, stilling his words. "I would prefer if we did not speak of our past."

"Why?"

"It is much too painful."

He winced. "There is so much that I need to tell you."

"Perhaps another time."

Colin hesitated before answering, "I can agree to that."

"Thank you," she murmured.

He offered his arm and smiled. "You do realize you won't get the plague if you touch me?"

"I am well aware."

"Then why do you always hesitate to take my arm?"

Arabella didn't dare admit that she always felt a fluttering in her stomach at his touch. "I do no such thing."

His smile grew. "Liar."

"It isn't polite to call a lady a liar," she chided as she placed her hand lightly on his sleeve.

"My apologies, my lady," he said, clearly amused.

Chapter Nine

Colin leaned lower in the saddle as he attempted to coax more speed out of his horse. He glanced over at his brother and saw that John was doing the same thing. Once they reached the top of the hill, Colin reined in his horse and his eyes roamed over his lands. He still couldn't quite believe this all belonged to him.

His brother's voice broke through his musings. "How did your visit with Lady Langdon and Arabella go?"

"It was uneventful," Colin muttered.

"Why was that?"

Colin frowned. "Arabella is so blasted stubborn."

"That's not surprising," John said. "She has been since we were little."

"I know, but it is quite vexing."

"How so?"

Colin adjusted the reins in his hand, then said, "Whenever I try to have a frank conversation about our past, she dismisses me out of hand."

"Why do you suppose that is?"

"I know not, but I do know that I hurt her deeply."

John gave him a knowing look. "That you did, brother."

"I want to make it up to her," Colin said.

"How do you propose to do that?"

Colin shrugged. "I'm not entirely sure, but I won't stop trying until my dying breath."

"You do realize that Mother is playing matchmaker between you two?"

"I am well aware."

John's gaze left his as he said, "I was hoping to speak to you about something important."

"I'm listening."

John paused. "I offered for Lady Marjorie Griffin and she accepted."

Colin stared at his brother in disbelief. "You are engaged?"

"I am."

"When did this happen?" Colin asked.

"Right before coming here."

"Why didn't you say anything before?"

John met his gaze. "I'm afraid it still doesn't seem real to me."

"Well, congratulations are in order!"

With a wince, John admitted, "I am not sure if congratulations are in order, or condolences."

"I'm afraid I don't understand."

John was silent for a long moment before saying, "Her brother caught us kissing in the gardens and demanded satisfaction. I decided to do the honorable thing and offer for Lady Marjorie."

"I see," Colin muttered. "But you must have some feelings for Lady Marjorie if you were kissing her."

"I do," John asserted. "She is unlike any young woman of my acquaintance."

"That is promising, then."

"It is, but I feel guilty and ashamed that I trapped her into marriage," John admitted.

"Have you spoken to her about this?"

John shook his head. "We haven't been able to be alone since we were caught in the gardens."

"Even when you offered for her?"

"I'm afraid not," John replied. "Her brother was present, and he was glaring at me the entire time."

"Lord Bristol is not known for his compassion in the House of Lords."

"I would agree. "

"When do you intend to tell Mother?"

John sighed. "I'm not sure. I know she will be terribly disappointed in me."

"I don't believe that will be the case," Colin contended. "You did the right thing, and you are marrying a woman that you hold in regard."

"What if Lady Marjorie grows to resent me for what I have done?"

Colin lifted his brow. "Did you force Lady Marjorie to kiss you?"

"No."

"Then she must hold you in some affection."

"I know she does, but that was before I forced her into a marriage."

"Perhaps you are just overthinking this," Colin said. "There is a chance that Lady Marjorie is feeling the same way as you are."

John's shoulder slumped slightly . "I am the third son of an earl and work as a barrister for my income," he said. "I daresay that Marjorie could have done much better than me."

"Does she have a dowry?"

"Ten thousand pounds."

Colin nodded in approval. "That is more than adequate to set up your own household."

"I agree, but I was hoping to reside in the London townhouse for the time being."

"You are always welcome, especially since I have no plans to visit Town until next Season."

"Thank you," John said.

"When do you intend to get married?"

"The banns should have just been posted, so I expect within the month."

Colin lifted his brow. "You aren't sure?"

"Sadly, a lot went unsaid after I offered for Marjorie," John shared. "I felt like I was being herded out of the room after she accepted."

"Why do you suppose that was?"

"Lord Bristol made it known that they had been hoping for a more auspicious match for Marjorie," John said.

"Regardless, this is a time for rejoicing," Colin attempted, "since you are engaged."

John looked heavenward. "I just wish I knew what Marjorie was thinking."

"You could always write her," he suggested. "It is perfectly acceptable for a man to write his betrothed."

"I suppose that could work."

"If you would like, you could have a rider personally deliver it to Lady Marjorie in London."

John grinned. "I'm afraid Mother made it rather clear that all the servants are previously occupied."

"I'm sure she will make an exception, given the circumstances."

With a bob of his head, John said, "I think a letter would work brilliantly."

"Perhaps you can have the letter delivered with flowers, as well."

"That would be a nice touch."

Colin saw his gamekeeper approaching him on foot. He put his hand up in greeting, and Burton did the same.

"I hope I am not intruding," Burton said.

"You are doing no such thing."

Burton came to a stop a few feet from him. "I'm afraid I bear bad news."

"Which is?"

"We found proof that the poacher has struck again," Burton said. "We found some blood on the ground and saw evidence of a carcass being dragged a short distance."

"Dragged?"

Burton nodded. "Yes, milord," he replied. "We have reason to believe that someone killed one of your deer."

"Blazes," Colin muttered.

"I have already taken the liberty of notifying the constable of the poaching, and he has assured me that he will make some inquiries."

"You were right to do so."

"I can assure you that me and my men will not rest until we find this poacher," Burton said firmly.

"I appreciate that."

Burton acknowledged John by the tipping of his head. "It is good to see you, Mr. Notley," he greeted.

"Likewise," John replied. "How is your family?"

"They are well, and I do thank you for asking." Burton shifted his gaze back towards Colin. "I will be sure to notify you right away once we catch the poacher."

"Thank you," Colin said.

"Good day to you both," Burton responded before he turned and walked away.

Colin's horse whinnied, drawing his attention. "It would appear that my horse is eager to stretch his legs," he remarked. "Shall we race back?"

"It won't be much of a race," John joked as he kicked his horse into a run.

WITH THE MORNING sun peeking through the trees, Arabella sat on a fallen log near the stream. It felt good to be alone, even though her thoughts kept constantly returning to Colin. She tried banishing him from her mind, but she didn't have the strength to do so.

What was she to do? Her heart was softening towards him, and she knew she was setting herself up for heartache. She couldn't let him in, not again. It was much safer to keep him at arm's length.

The sound of rustling bushes nearby drew her attention. She quickly rose and stepped closer to her horse. She hadn't made it into her saddle before the young boy from the village emerged from the bushes, holding a dead pheasant in his hand.

"Peter?" Arabella questioned.

Peter's face grew white as he came to an abrupt halt.

She glanced down at the pheasant in his hand and realization dawned. "Are you poaching on Lord Barrett's land?"

He hesitated for a moment before admitting, "I am."

"Do you not know the consequences for poaching?"

"I do."

"Then why would you risk going to jail?"

Peter's eyes grew wide. "I can't go to jail," he said. "I have to take care of my mother."

"Does your mother know you are poaching?"

He shook his head. "She doesn't."

"How is that possible?"

"She works long hours at the milliner's, and she leaves for work before the sun comes up," Peter said. "Sometimes she doesn't come home until after sundown."

"If that is the case, then surely she makes enough wages for you not to poach."

"Her wages barely cover the rent," Peter explained.

"There must be another way to make an honest wage."

Peter shook his head. "I've tried, but no one will hire me."

A Tangled Wreath

"Why not?"

A pained look came to his face. "Ye wouldn't understand," he said.

Arabella could hear the pain in his voice, and she found compassion swelling up inside of her. "I shall speak to my grandmother and see if we can get you hired on at her manor."

His eyes grew wide. "You would do that for me?"

"I would, but you must promise me that you will stop poaching."

"I will have no need if I can make an honest wage."

"That is good."

Peter shifted the pheasant to his other hand as he nervously asked, "Are you going to tell Lord Barrett?"

"I see no reason to do so, assuming you promise me that you will stop."

A relieved look came to his face. "Thank you, miss," he gushed. "That is most kind of you."

She pointed towards the pheasant. "Will that be enough to feed you and your mother today?"

"It will," he confirmed.

"I am pleased to hear that."

Peter puffed out his chest as he admitted, "I killed a deer yesterday."

Her brow lifted. "You killed a deer?"

"I did," he replied. "I used my father's pistol to shoot it."

Finding herself curious, she asked, "Where is your father?"

Peter grew quiet. "He was a soldier, and he died fighting in the war."

"I am sorry," she replied. "How long ago did he pass away?"

"Four years ago."

"That is a long time to be without a father."

The boy squared his thin shoulders. "Last time he came

home on leave, he made me promise that I would look after my mother."

"That is most admirable of you."

"It is my duty to care for her."

Arabella sighed. "I can respect that, but I am sure that Lord Barrett's gamekeeper will notice that a deer has gone missing," she said.

"But he has so many deer on his lands."

"That hardly matters," Arabella replied. "It is still stealing."

Lowering his gaze to the ground, Peter admitted, "I sold the deer to Mr. Franks."

"Who is he?"

"The innkeeper."

"I see," she said. "Did he ask where you got the deer?"

Peter shifted nervously in his stance. "He has never asked before."

"You've killed more than one deer?"

"I have," he revealed. "The money I get from selling the deer feeds us for the whole week."

Arabella stepped away from her horse. "You can't keep going on as you have been. Lord Barrett is aware that someone is poaching on his lands."

"He is?"

"Yes, and if you are caught, you won't be able to take care of your mother any longer."

The boy kicked at a rock on the ground. "But what will we eat?"

"Are you familiar with Lady Langdon's manor?"

He bobbed his head.

"I want you to come by tomorrow and we shall see about acquiring you a job," she said. "Furthermore, I am sure our cook will have some bread to spare for you."

Peter smiled. "Thank you," he responded enthusiastically.

The sound of a horse whinnying in the distance drew both

of their attention. She turned back to Peter and said, "You need to go."

Needing no further encouragement, Peter ran deeper into the woodlands and disappeared from her view within moments.

Arabella led her horse over to the fallen log and used it to mount. Once she was secure on her side saddle, she urged her horse forward through the familiar path.

She had just exited the woodlands when she saw Colin riding towards her. She reined in her horse and waited for him to do the same.

"Good morning," he greeted.

She brought a smile to her lips. "Good morning."

"I see that you are still an early riser."

"I find that I have a lot on my mind."

His eyes left hers and scanned the woodlands. "My gamekeeper has informed me that a deer has been poached."

"That is awful." She felt bad for holding information from Colin, but she didn't dare confess that Peter was the poacher.

"I would feel more comfortable if you would avoid the woodlands until after the poacher has been arrested."

"I do not believe that to be necessary."

Colin brought his gaze back to meet hers. "Is that so?"

"I can take care of myself."

"Do be serious."

Arabella tilted her chin. "I am," she replied. "If it would appease you, I will bring a muff pistol on my rides with me."

"I would prefer if you didn't ride unescorted, at least for the time being."

"You have no say in that."

His jaw clenched. "Poachers are notoriously dangerous men, and I do not believe they would hesitate to harm you."

"I understand, but I believe I shall take my chances."

"Bella—"

She put her hand up, stilling his words. "I do thank you for your concern, but it is quite unnecessary."

Colin frowned as he stared at her for a long moment. "Why do you even own a muff pistol?" he finally asked.

"The streets of London are also rather dangerous for a young woman."

"Just promise me that you will use caution when you enter these woodlands," he requested.

She bobbed her head. "I can agree to that."

"Thank you." He hesitated before asking, "May I escort you home?"

"That won't be necessary, but I do thank you kindly for the offer."

Colin smiled. "Will I be seeing you later, when the children from the orphanage come to decorate the two trees?"

"I wouldn't dream of missing the excitement."

"Nor I."

"Will your mother be joining us?"

"I believe so."

"Wonderful," Arabella said.

Colin looked unsure, which was in stark contrast to how he usually appeared. "Would you care to go ice skating with me tomorrow?"

Arabella pressed her lips together, delaying her response. As much as she wanted to say yes, she didn't dare do that to herself.

"Before you refuse me," Colin started, "just think of how much fun we used to have ice skating together."

"Colin…"

"It will be like old times."

Despite her reservations, she found herself saying, "It does sound like fun."

"Is that a yes, then?"

Arabella wasn't quite sure, but it appeared as if Colin was holding his breath in anticipation of her response. "It is."

Colin smiled. "You have made me immensely happy, Bella."

"Then my work here is done," she teased. "I should be going. I intend to join my grandmother for breakfast."

"I shall see you later, then."

"Yes, you shall," she said before kicking her horse into a run.

Arabella scolded herself for agreeing to go ice skating with Colin. But it was just one outing with him; surely, there could be no harm that would come from that.

Chapter Ten

Colin was elated as he raced back to his manor. He felt like he had secured his first real victory with Arabella, and he knew that was no small feat. She was as stubborn as she was beautiful.

He reined in his horse in front of the stable and dismounted. As he extended the reins towards a waiting groom, his brother stepped outside.

"Why are you smiling like a fool?" John asked.

"Am I?"

John eyed him curiously. "You just came from seeing Arabella, didn't you?"

"I did."

"Something must have happened between you two."

Colin nodded. "She agreed to go ice skating with me tomorrow."

"Well done, Brother!" John praised. "Did you have to grovel?"

"I did not."

"Ah," John said. "Arabella must have taken pity on you, then."

Colin chuckled. "Perhaps, but I am not complaining."

John gestured towards the manor. "I believe you have earned your breakfast this morning."

"That I did," Colin replied.

They started walking back towards the manor. "I sent a messenger off this morning," John revealed.

"You did?"

"I ordered him to remain at Lady Marjorie's townhouse until she penned a reply," John shared.

"That is rather brazen, is it not?"

"I hate not knowing her feelings on the matter."

"Were you honest and forthright in your letter?"

"I was," John confirmed.

"Then you have nothing to fear."

John glanced over at him. "I truly doubt that," he said. "I counted over a hundred ways that this ends poorly for me."

"Only a hundred?" Colin joked.

"I'm afraid I stopped counting after that."

"That was probably wise."

As they approached the door, Dickson opened it, and they stepped into the entry hall. John turned to face Colin. "I couldn't help but wonder if I should have delivered the note myself."

"How do you think that would have been received?"

John winced. "I'm not sure."

"Then you were wise to send a messenger."

The words had barely left his mouth when his mother shouted from the top of the stairs. "You are *engaged?*"

"Botheration," John muttered.

Their mother descended the stairs, brandishing a morning newspaper in her hand, her eyes focused on John. "When were you going to tell me that you were engaged to Lady Marjorie?"

John put his hands up in front of him. "In due time…"

"In due time?" she repeated. "But I am your mother!"

"Perhaps we should have this conversation in the drawing

room," Colin suggested in a low voice, "where there aren't any inquisitive ears."

"Yes," their mother agreed. "That would be for the best."

No one spoke as they walked the short distance to the drawing room, and Colin closed the door behind him.

Their mother crossed her arms over her chest. "How could you post the banns without telling me that you offered for Lady Marjorie?"

"I didn't mean to hurt you," John started.

"What was your intention?" she asked.

John pursed his lips together. "I'm afraid my engagement was rather sudden."

Their mother gasped. "You didn't compromise her, did you?"

"Define compromise?" John asked slowly.

"How could you?" she asked as she sat on the settee. "I thought I raised you better than this."

"You did," John rushed to say. "Marjorie's brother caught us kissing in the garden and demanded satisfaction."

"He challenged you to a duel?"

"He did, but I did the honorable thing and offered for Marjorie," John explained.

Their mother turned her gaze towards Colin. "Did you know about this?"

"I only just found out," Colin replied.

With a frown on her lips, their mother asked, "Do you even hold any affection for this girl?"

"I do," John replied.

"I suppose that will have to do," she responded. "I don't even know anything about Lady Marjorie. Is she accomplished?"

"She is," John confirmed. "She attended Mrs. Harper's Seminary School for Ladies."

"That is a prestigious boarding school."

"That it is."

"Does she have a sense of humor?" their mother asked.

John bobbed his head. "She is quite witty."

"How did you two even become acquainted?"

"She is dear friends with Cousin Lucy," John explained. "I met Marjorie at one of her soirées this Season."

Their mother looked put out. "Yet, this is the first I have heard of her."

"I was trying to find the right opportunity to tell you."

"The right opportunity?"

John gave her a look. "I couldn't very well just blurt out that I was engaged."

"Whyever not?"

"I was afraid you would be disappointed in me," John said.

His mother's face softened. "All I have ever wanted was for you to be happy." She paused. "Are you?"

"I am," John admitted. "Marjorie is precisely the type of woman I have always envisioned that I would marry."

"Then we should celebrate," she said, rising. "We will have champagne with our breakfast."

"Isn't it rather early to be drinking?" Colin questioned, amused.

She turned her gaze towards him. "Don't be such a killjoy," she said with a wave of her hand. "It is not every day that one of my sons gets engaged."

"No, it is not," Colin agreed.

His mother walked over to the door and opened it. "Dickson!" she exclaimed. "Will you see to some champagne for our breakfast?"

After she closed the door, she stepped over to John and patted his cheek. "I am so proud of you," she said. "I cannot wait to meet Lady Marjorie."

"I can assure you that you won't be disappointed," John expressed. "She is a remarkable young woman."

His mother smiled. "When is the wedding?"

A Tangled Wreath

John glanced nervously at Colin before replying, "I am not entirely sure."

Her smile dimmed. "What does that mean?"

"There is some confusion about the date we are to be wed."

"Confusion? How?"

John sighed. "Marjorie's brother is tasked with posting the banns, but he has not informed me of having done so."

"Then you must ask him," their mother encouraged.

"I wrote a letter last night to Marjorie, and I'm having a messenger deliver it to her today," John explained. "With any luck, she will notify me of the date."

"How romantic," their mother said. "Writing notes can be rather scandalous."

"There is nothing scandalous about my note," John defended.

"You are no fun," she joked. "Soon both of my boys will be wed, and I will have a horde of grandchildren to spoil."

Colin furrowed his brow. "I have no intention of marrying any time soon."

"We shall see," their mother said.

"I am in earnest," Colin pressed.

"Of course you are, my dear," she responded in a complacent tone. "Shall we adjourn to the breakfast parlor for some champagne?"

Colin opened the door. "After you, Mother," he encouraged, standing to the side.

AS ARABELLA DESCENDED THE STAIRS, she saw her grandmother standing in the entry hall speaking to Moore. She came to a stop in front of them and waited to be acknowledged.

Her grandmother turned to face her. "Did you have a good rest?"

"I did."

"I am pleased to hear that, because the manor will soon be filled with boisterous children," her grandmother declared.

"It sounds wonderful."

"Today will be a most joyous occasion."

Arabella couldn't help but return her infectious smile. "I am pleased to be a part of it."

"Come," her grandmother encouraged, "I want to show you the saloon."

As they entered the saloon, Arabella saw that tables lined in the center of the room with all types of decorations for the trees.

Her grandmother pointed at the tables. "We have sweetmeats, almonds, raisins, fruits and toys," she said.

"How many children are coming?"

"Sixteen." Her grandmother glanced over at the tree Arabella had selected. "It is not too late to remove your tree from the saloon."

"Whyever would we do that?"

"Because it looks rather pitiful next to the tree that Colin selected."

Arabella frowned, knowing her grandmother made a valid point, but she didn't dare admit it. There was nothing wrong with her tree. It may not look as splendid as Colin's tree, but it would provide the children with ample opportunity to decorate.

"I think the children will enjoy the opportunity to decorate two trees," Arabella said.

A twinkle came to her grandmother's eyes. "You remind me so much of my Aunt Victoria."

"How so?"

"She was born in Germany, but her family moved to England when her father was assigned as the ambassador," her grandmother explained. "She was quite the beauty in her day, or so I have been told, and she took the London Season by storm."

"I fail to see how we are similar," Arabella remarked.

Her grandmother laughed. "She was stubborn, and she insisted on having her manor filled with trees for Christmas. It always smelled liked an evergreen forest in her home."

"That does sound delightful."

"Victoria outlived three husbands and died when she was eighty-five," her grandmother continued. "Her first two husbands died from heart failure."

"How awful," Arabella said. "How did her third husband die?"

"He was trampled by a horse when he crossed a busy street in London."

Arabella stared at her grandmother. "What a terrible story!"

Her grandmother gave her an innocent look. "I never said it was a pleasant ending for her third husband."

"Regardless, I would have hoped for a happier ending for her."

"Very few people live a life without tragedy to accompany it."

Arabella walked over to her tree and ran her fingers over a green branch. "Wouldn't it be grand to have a life that was filled without anguish or sorrow?"

"Then how would you learn and grow?" her grandmother asked.

"That may be true, but it would save me from heartache," Arabella replied. "I feel my heart is too broken to ever heal."

Her grandmother walked over to her and laid a hand on her sleeve. "I have discovered that the most beautiful things have dents and scratches. It's proof that they have had a life worth living."

"Thank you for that, Grandmother."

She smiled. "You are still young, and you have a bright future ahead of you."

"We both know that is not true."

"Do not sell yourself short," her grandmother encouraged. "You have no idea what lays ahead of you."

"I think we both know I will end up as a spinster."

"There are worse things," her grandmother said, giving her a knowing look. "Besides, if you truly wanted to marry, you could always accept Lord Eastwood's offer."

Arabella shuddered. "I think not."

"Then you must go forward and embrace the glorious person that you are."

"I daresay you are biased."

Her grandmother lowered her hand. "I always have been when it has come to you," she said. "You managed to touch my heart from the moment you were born."

"I am lucky to have a grandmother such as you."

"We are lucky to have one another."

Arabella nodded. "I can agree to that…" Her words trailed off when she saw mistletoe hanging above the doorway. "Why is that there?"

Her grandmother followed her gaze. "As I have said before, your grandfather was rather fond of mistletoe."

"But he isn't here anymore."

"No, but you are," her grandmother responded, "and I couldn't resist."

A long clock chimed in the corner, alerting them of the time.

Her grandmother clasped her hands together. "How exciting!" she exclaimed. "The children will be here shortly."

As Arabella turned back towards her tree, Colin's amused voice came from the doorway. "I still contend that tree will frighten the children."

"It is not as terrible as you claim," she defended.

A Tangled Wreath

Colin closed the distance between them. "We shall see which tree the children will prefer soon enough, won't we?"

"We shall," she said, trying to pretend that his nearness didn't affect her. But it did. Greatly.

He smiled, a charming one that drew her attention towards his mouth. "You look lovely today, Bella."

"That is kind of you to say."

"It is merely the truth."

Diane stepped into the room and embraced Arabella's grandmother. "What a blessed day!" she exclaimed as she stepped back.

"That it is." Her grandmother gestured towards the tables with both hands. "I believe we have enough decorations to decorate two trees."

Colin stepped away from her and approached the tables. "I daresay that you have enough to decorate your whole manor here."

Diane stepped over to Arabella and looked the tree up and down. "This is a most unique tree, is it not?"

"It is."

"It is so ugly that I find it charming," Diane said.

Arabella frowned. "It is not that bad."

Diane turned to face her. "The most important thing is that you love it."

"I do."

"Then that is all that matters," Diane remarked.

Colin chuckled. "You are giving her false hope, Mother."

Diane swatted at his sleeve. "Do not be cruel, Colin," she chided. "Arabella selected this tree for a specific reason, and we must respect that."

"You are right." Colin turned his attention towards her. "I do apologize for criticizing this… interesting tree."

"I accept your apology," Arabella said.

Diane nodded in approval. "If you will excuse me, I am going to sample the sweetmeats before the children arrive."

As his mother stepped over to the tables, Colin remarked, "My mother is quite fond of sweetmeats."

"It is rather thoughtful of you to accompany your mother here."

"I wouldn't dare miss seeing the excitement on the children's faces as they decorate my tree."

"You mean 'our trees'," she amended.

Colin smirked. "I spoke correctly."

"You are a pompous jackanapes," she muttered.

"Language, my dear," he teased. "We wouldn't want the children to overhear you saying such wicked things."

Her lips twitched. "Remind me again why I am friends with you?"

He sobered a bit. "Are we friends?" he asked, his eyes roaming over her face.

"I suppose we are."

A slow smile spread across his mouth and spilled into his eyes. "I am pleased to hear that."

"That is, assuming you stop making fun of my tree."

Colin made a face. "I'm afraid I can't agree to that," he said. "It is just awful."

Before she could reply, the sounds of the children could be heard coming from the entry hall, announcing their arrival.

Chapter Eleven

Colin remained rooted in his spot as he watched girls of all ages walk into the saloon. They wore plain frocks and had their hair neatly done.

As Lady Langdon and his mother rushed over to greet them, he leaned closer to Arabella and asked, "What is the plan?"

"Whatever do you mean?" she asked.

"I am unsure what I should be doing right now."

Arabella turned her head, their faces only inches apart. "Just smile and enjoy yourself."

"I can do that," Colin replied, pasting on a grin.

Her eyes darted to his lips. "You might want to work on your smile."

"What is wrong with this smile?"

"It looks as though you are grimacing."

"That is just ridiculous," he replied. "There is nothing wrong with my smile."

Arabella shrugged one shoulder. "It was merely a suggestion," she said. "There is no reason to take offense."

"I can assure you that I was not offended. Just curious."

"I am glad, because none was intended."

Colin was enjoying being so near to Arabella, and he was pleased that she had not moved to create more distance between them. He just needed something clever to say to keep her engaged.

While he was thinking of something to say, Arabella asked, "What is the punishment for poachers?"

"Pardon?" He had not been expecting that question.

"What happens when a poacher is caught?"

"He is arrested and carted off to jail."

Arabella pressed her lips together, clearly displeased by his response. "What if the poacher is just trying to feed his family?"

"Regardless, it is a crime to hunt on someone else's land, and it has to be dealt with via swift retribution."

"Why is that?"

"If word ever got out that I was lenient about hunting on my lands, then poachers would arrive in hordes and kill off all the wildlife," Colin said. "I would be left with nothing."

"I understand," she said softly.

"Arresting poachers brings me no pleasure," he assured her, "but they are stealing from me."

"Forget I said anything."

He cocked his head. "Why did you say something?"

"I suppose I feel some sympathy for the villagers who go hungry, leaving them little choice but to poach."

"How do you know it is someone from the village?"

"Who else could it be?"

"It is not uncommon for gangs of men to descend on an estate and kill a large amount of game," he said.

"That is awful."

"They raid an area, stripping it bare of all the game," Colin continued. "Then they cart it off to London where it would fetch a hefty price."

"Do you believe a gang of men are poaching from you?"

A Tangled Wreath

"I do not," Colin said with a shake of his head. "The evidence does not support that conclusion."

With a pointed look, Arabella remarked, "Perhaps we should discuss this later. We are being rude to our guests."

His gaze left hers and he saw that the girls were already starting to decorate his tree, hushed excitement in their voices.

Arabella glanced back at her tree and sighed. "It would appear that the girls are not interested in decorating this tree."

"You don't know that."

Arabella huffed. "I overheard one of the girls saying that this tree looked sad."

"Then we shall decorate it."

"Truly?" she asked.

Colin nodded. "I haven't decorated a tree in ages," he said. "It would be fun."

A bright smile came to Arabella's lips. "I agree."

"We will need some sweetmeats and almonds," he said. "I'm hoping the branches will support the extra weight." He smiled to let her know that he was teasing.

She gave him an exasperated look. "I am confident that the tree can hold the weight of sweetmeats and almonds."

"Perhaps, but one cannot be too careful," he joked.

Colin walked over to the table and grabbed a few bags of almonds. As he started walking back to the tree, a young girl stopped him and asked, "Why are you decorating *that* tree?"

"Because every tree deserves to be decorated."

The girl lowered her voice. "But that tree is ugly."

He smiled as he crouched down. "Beauty is in the eye of the beholder," he said.

She didn't appear convinced as she turned her attention back towards the tree. "I'm not sure if that is true."

Reaching into his waistcoat pocket, he pulled out a coin. "If you help me decorate the tree, you can have this farthing."

Her eyes went wide. "Are you in earnest?"

"I am, but you can't tell anyone I bribed you to help."

"Why?"

He pointed at Arabella, who was busy placing sweetmeats on the tree. "That young woman thinks her tree is the most beautiful tree in the whole world."

"Does she need spectacles?"

He chuckled. "No, but you need to pretend you like the tree."

The young girl bobbed her head vehemently. "I can do that."

"Good," he replied, extending her the coin. "I do appreciate your help."

As she clutched the coin in her little hand, the girl said, "I am going to get some toys to put on the tree. It might make it less sad."

"That's a good idea," he agreed, rising. The girl ran towards the tables, and Colin walked back over to the tree. "I was able to recruit one of the girls to help decorate," he revealed.

Arabella looked at him in surprise. "You did?"

"Yes." He was pleased when the young girl appeared by his side. "She has offered to help."

Arabella smiled at her. "What is your name?"

"Sarah," she replied.

"I do appreciate your help in decorating this tree," Arabella said. "We could use all the help we can get."

Sarah returned Arabella's smile. "I think toys will help with the gaps where the branches should be."

"I would agree," Arabella replied.

Sarah went and placed a few toys onto the tree branches. "This tree is so beautiful," she gushed. "At first it looks ugly, but it looks much better the closer you get."

"You truly believe so?"

Sarah bobbed her head. "Yes, and I came to that conclusion entirely on my own," she said. "No one told me to tell you that."

A Tangled Wreath

Colin cleared his throat, drawing the girl's attention. "Perhaps you should go get some more almonds to put on the tree."

"That is a good idea," Sarah said before she hurried over to the table.

Arabella arched an eyebrow. "That was quite the performance."

"It was," he responded, pretending to feign interest in the tree.

She stepped closer to him, keeping her voice low. "Did you bribe that girl in some way to lie to me about the tree?"

He turned to face her. "I may have given her an incentive to help decorate it."

"Meaning?"

"I paid her a farthing," he admitted with a wince.

To his surprise, Arabella started giggling. "That is awful of you," she said, bringing her hand up to her mouth. "You shouldn't have done such a thing."

He stepped back as Sarah approached with a handful of almonds. "If we place the bags of almonds on the tree, I should be able to convince the other girls to eat them."

Arabella set her hand on his sleeve and mouthed, "Thank you."

He smiled in response and placed his hand over hers, enjoying their private moment.

Lady Langdon spoke up from across the room. "Arabella," she said. "May I see you for a moment?"

"Of course," Arabella replied, slipping her hand out from under his.

As she walked away, he couldn't help but notice the smile forming on Lady Langdon's lips.

STANDING IN THE ENTRY HALL, Arabella let out a sigh of relief once the last orphan departed from the manor, each with a toy in their hand. They had spent hours decorating the trees, and after they had admired them, they partook of the sweets that each bore. Now her feet hurt, and she couldn't wait until she could take a long, relaxing soak.

Colin came to stand next to her. "That was an enriching experience."

"It was," she readily agreed.

"The children seemed taken by the toys that they received."

"That they did." Arabella turned to face him. "That was sweet of you to lift the girls up to reach the higher branches."

Colin shrugged. "It was of little consequence."

"True, but it made the little girls smile."

"Then my work here is done," he said, performing an overexaggerated bow.

She smiled. "You are incorrigible."

"That's better than being a jackanapes," he said with mirth in his voice.

"True," she replied.

Her grandmother interrupted, "Shall we begin to dress for dinner?"

Arabella put a hand on her stomach. "I don't think I can eat another thing. I had entirely too many sweetmeats."

"But we mustn't be rude to our guests," her grandmother asserted. "Colin and Diane accepted our invitation to dine with us."

"Quite frankly, I feel the same as Arabella," Colin admitted. "I ate entirely too many sweets."

Diane spoke up as she approached them. "As did I."

"Thank heavens," Arabella's grandmother said. "I was dreading the thought of eating another bite, but I didn't dare say anything."

Colin met Arabella's gaze and asked, "Would you care to

A Tangled Wreath

take a turn around the garden with me? I find myself in need of fresh air after being in the same room for so long."

"That sounds delightful."

He offered his arm, and she accepted it. As they walked towards the rear of the manor, he asked, "Did you enjoy yourself today?"

"I did," she replied. "I adore children."

"As do I."

"Perhaps it wouldn't be terrible if Augusta had children," Arabella remarked. "It would finally give me the siblings that I so desperately craved as a child."

"I hadn't realized you felt that way."

"My parents doted on me something fierce, but I still wished that I had a playmate," she said. "The only child my age was the cook's daughter, and my father forbade me from playing with her."

"He forbade you?"

"He did," she replied. "He didn't think it was proper for me to play with a servant's child. Instead, I spent most of my time with a nursemaid."

"That must have been rather lonely."

"It was, but I shouldn't complain," she said.

"I didn't think you were complaining."

They departed from the manor, and a footman discreetly followed them outside. The cold air hit her cheeks and she shuddered a little as she adjusted her shawl.

"Are you cold?" he asked.

"It feels refreshing, especially after being indoors all afternoon."

Colin nodded. "I feel the same way," he said. "I have never enjoyed being cooped up inside."

Arabella glanced over at him. "How are you feeling since the other night?" she asked. "Have you had any other episodes?"

"I have not."

"May I ask what triggers them?"

Colin frowned. "It depends, really," he said. "Sometimes it is just an image that comes to my mind, or I will hear a noise that takes me back to the peninsula."

"I'm sorry to hear that."

"I saw some terrible things over there, but I also formed solidarity with my fellow soldiers. I knew I needed to trust them with my life to survive." He paused. "They are still serving, offering up their lives if necessary, and I'm sitting in a manor, learning about the latest farming techniques."

Colin reached down and rubbed his leg. "The only thing I was able to take home with me is an injury that marks me as a cripple."

"You are hardly a cripple," she argued. "Your limp is barely discernable."

"I daresay we must agree to disagree on that." Colin led her to a bench and assisted her as she sat down. "I assume you are tired of being on your feet."

"I am."

Colin claimed the seat next to her, but he maintained proper distance. "It is quite lovely out here."

Arabella nodded. "When I was younger, I used to come and sit here for hours," she said. "I dreamed of what my life would be like."

"And did your dreams come to pass?"

She laughed. "Heavens, no," she declared. "I have two broken engagements, and I can assure you that was never part of my plan."

"Those events do not define you."

"I feel as if they do," Arabella said, lowering her gaze to her lap. "I have failed at even the simplest task."

"Which is?"

"Finding a husband."

"Is that all you want?" he asked. "Just to secure a husband?"

A Tangled Wreath

Arabella brought her gaze back up. "A husband brings security."

"But if you marry the wrong one, it also brings forth heartache and sorrow."

"I am well aware," she said. "That is why I turned down Lord Eastwood's offer, even though I know my father will be furious at my decision."

"He may surprise you."

She huffed. "I have no doubt that he will lecture me on becoming a drain to the household's expenses."

"You're not giving yourself enough credit, Bella."

"How so?"

He held her gaze intently as he remarked, "You are a beautiful young woman, and any man would be lucky to have you as his wife."

But he'd chosen otherwise.

Arabella abruptly rose, causing Colin to rise awkwardly. "We should go back inside," she said curtly.

"Why are you running from me?" Colin asked.

"I'm not."

Colin gave her a knowing look. "You most certainly are. Why is that?"

"I just find some topics to be rather uncomfortable to discuss with you."

"Such as?"

Arabella pressed her lips together, then said, "You said any man would be lucky to have me for a wife, but you rejected me yourself."

"I did, but it was for your own good."

"Pardon me if I don't believe that," she remarked, turning to leave.

Colin put a hand on her arm to still her retreat. "Please don't go," he said. "Allow me to explain."

Despite her reservations, she found herself curious about what he had to say. "You have one minute."

Running a hand through his hair, Colin said, "I have practiced this speech hundreds of times, but I'm afraid I find myself at a loss for words."

"Then perhaps we should go inside."

"No," he said firmly. "I will find the words. Just please give me a moment."

The small plea in his voice made her pause. "Go ahead, then."

Colin met her gaze. "When you accepted my offer of marriage, I was the happiest man alive," he revealed, "but I knew that I was being terribly unfair to you."

"How so?"

"I was serving in the army, and I intended to make a career out of it," he explained. "I had no idea if I would survive each battle, much less the war."

"I was aware of this."

Colin took a step closer to her. "I wanted more for you," he said. "You deserved a husband that never left your side."

"I agreed to your offer, knowing you would be gone for months or years."

"But it wasn't fair of me to ask that of you," he said. "Furthermore, you would have been expected to live on an officer's salary. It was a far cry from the life you were used to, and I knew that I couldn't do that to you."

"So you decided for me?"

"I did," he replied. "I did what was best for you."

Arabella saw the crestfallen look on Colin's face and knew that he was in earnest, but breaking their engagement hadn't been fair of him.

"Thank you for explaining your reasons, but you were wrong in doing so," she said. "I would have waited for you until my last breath."

"But I might never have come home."

"Then I would have treasured the time that we did have

together." She took a step closer to him. "I'm afraid you underestimated how much I loved you."

"Bella…"

"You made your choice, Colin," she said firmly. "Just so you know, I accepted your offer because of *you*. Not because of your prospects."

He winced a little. "You deserved better than me."

"You're right," she agreed with a bob of her head. "I deserved someone who would have fought to keep me."

Reaching for her hand, he gently encompassed it in his own and asked, "Pray tell, how can I make this right between us?"

"What is it that you want from me?" she asked, searching his eyes.

"I want another chance with you."

Tears pricked the back of her eyes. "Do you know how hard it was to go on after you ended our engagement?" she asked, slipping her hand out of his. "You took my heart, my trust, and misused them terribly."

"I am so incredibly sorry for the hurt that I caused you, but my circumstances have changed." He hesitated. "I've changed."

"I'm sorry, Colin, but that is a poor excuse."

Arabella turned to leave, but his voice stopped her. "We are still friends, are we not?"

"Yes," she replied. "But that is all I can give for now."

His brow lifted. "For now?" he asked. "Are you telling me that there might be a chance for us?"

A tear rolled down her cheek and she reached up to wipe it away. "Even after everything that has transpired between us, my traitorous heart still leaps at the sight of you."

His next words were gentle. "Then I shall strive to be patient."

"I can't promise anything," she responded softly.

"I know, and I wouldn't expect you to."

A sudden gust of wind made her shiver. "It would be best if we returned to the manor, where it is warm."

"Allow me to escort you," he said, offering his arm.

As they walked back towards the manor, Arabella chided herself. Why had she been so brazen to admit she still had feelings for him? She knew she would always love him, but could she ever trust him again?

Dear Margarette

Langdon Hall, Maidstone
December 24, 1815

How I wish you were here and could have seen the happy faces of the orphans as they decorated the trees! It was a momentous occasion, and Colin even convinced one of the orphans to help trim Arabella's tree. It didn't look quite as sad once it was properly adorned.

I have seen a change come over Arabella. She is softening her stance towards Colin, but I am not even sure she recognizes it. She is quite stubborn, much like my late husband was. I know she is protecting her heart, but I fear that she is foolish in doing so. There is so much potential for joy when you open your heart to another.

Colin and Arabella have been taking walks in the gardens and I have been shamelessly watching them from the warmth of the drawing room. It is encouraging, but how I wish you were here to help me with my matchmaking attempts. You always seem to know the right thing to do.

I do hope you are having a pleasant Christmastide. The weather is entirely too cold for my liking, but that hasn't stopped Arabella from riding every morning. She reminds me so much of my Sophia, and I'm afraid I have grown rather nostalgic.

I hope this letter finds you well, and I look forward to your thoughts on the matter.

Yours fondly,
Esther

Chapter Twelve

Colin sat in an armchair and attempted to focus on the book in his hand, but his thoughts kept turning to Arabella. She'd given him hope for a future between them, and he was elated at the prospect. Now he just had to prove that he was the man for her.

But how in the blazes was he going to do that?

He could buy her anything her heart desired, but he didn't think that would sway her. She wanted more, deserved more. Somehow, he needed to show her precisely how much she meant to him, but he was at a loss for how to do so. He had no trouble commanding a group of men, but the thought of confessing his love was terrifying.

His brother stepped into the room and headed straight to the drink cart. After he poured himself a drink, he brought it up to his lips and said, "The messenger still has not returned with Marjorie's reply."

"Is that a problem?"

John took a sip of his drink. "What is taking her so long to write a blasted note?" he mumbled.

Colin leaned back in his chair and asked, "How long did it take for you to write your letter to her?"

"All night."

"Then you should grant her the same courtesy."

John sat on the settee. "You are being entirely too reasonable this morning," he grumbled.

"Aren't I always?"

"No," John replied. "Sometimes you can be downright cantankerous."

"Perhaps, but I find myself in a tolerable mood this morning."

John gave him a look. "Did something happen with Arabella?"

A smile tugged at Colin's lips. "We had a frank conversation last night after the children from the orphanage left, and I learned that she still holds me in some affection."

"That's wonderful!" John declared. "When's the wedding?"

Colin put his hand up. "I said that she holds me in *some* affection," he said. "I never said she was willing to marry me."

"But you will persuade her?"

"I hope so, but Arabella can be quite stubborn."

"As can you."

"I am well aware, which is why I don't intend to stop wooing her until I have convinced her to be my bride."

"How do you plan to do that?"

Colin sighed. "That is a really good question, and I am open to ideas."

John placed his drink onto the table. "You could buy her flowers," he suggested.

"I don't think that will impress her."

"Jewelry, then?"

Colin shook his head. "I have already thought of that, but I don't believe it's what Arabella needs or wants."

"You could buy her a horse," John proposed. "She loves riding."

A Tangled Wreath

"That she does, but that is a rather presumptuous gift," he said. "Don't you think?"

John shrugged. "I shouldn't be the only one tossing around ideas."

Colin rose from his chair and walked over to the drink cart. As he picked up the decanter, he said, "We are going ice skating this afternoon."

"With any luck, you will be engaged soon after," John joked.

Colin chuckled as he poured himself a drink. "I do not believe so, but that is a pleasant enough thought," he responded. "You could always join us."

"Frankly, I would rather be anywhere else."

"It could get your mind off Lady Marjorie."

John groaned. "Why did you have to bring her up?" he asked. "It was nice to have a momentary reprieve."

"You poor, tortured soul," Colin teased.

"Thank you," John said, reaching for his drink. "I am glad someone is finally able to see what I am forced to endure."

Colin picked up his glass and took a sip. "You are fortunate enough to be engaged to the woman you care for."

"But I am unsure of her affection, and that is agonizing."

"It'll all work out."

John huffed. "Are you a fortune teller now?"

"No, but I am trying to stay positive," Colin said.

"That doesn't sound like you," John remarked. "You are generally a naysayer."

Dickson stepped into the room with a tray in his hands and turned to John. "A letter was just delivered for you, sir."

John jumped up and put his drink on the table, then hurried over to the butler and picked up the letter.

"It's from Marjorie!" John exclaimed, staring at the folded piece of paper.

"Are you going to read it?" Colin asked, bemused.

John unfolded the paper and started reading. After a long moment, he lowered the paper and declared, "She cares for me!"

"That is wonderful news!"

"It is," John said. "She informed me that the wedding is to be in three weeks' time and her family will be hosting a luncheon after the ceremony."

"Where will the wedding be?"

"At her brother's country estate in Kent," John shared. "They have a chapel on their lands and the vicar is their second cousin."

"You will need to inform Mother straightaway," Colin urged.

"I shall," John said, folding the note and slipping it into the pocket of his blue jacket. "She will be thrilled by the news!"

"I have no doubt."

John smiled broadly. "I am engaged!" he exclaimed.

"Yes, you are," Colin said, returning his smile.

"I'm marrying the girl of my choice, despite the unorthodox way of going about it."

"I am truly happy for you."

Their mother stepped into the library. "Why is John announcing he is engaged?" she asked. "I thought that was already established?"

"He just received a letter from Marjorie, and she confessed her undying love to him," Colin revealed.

Their mother clasped her hands together. "How wonderful!" she said, turning towards John. "I am so happy for you!"

"Thank you," John responded. "Frankly, it doesn't quite seem real that I won Marjorie's affection."

"A marriage with a foundation of love is all that I have ever wanted for you." Their mother glanced over at Colin. "For both of you."

A Tangled Wreath

"I am still a long way from securing Arabella's love," Colin said.

"I doubt that," their mother remarked. "I have seen the way her eyes light up when you walk into the room."

"Regardless, I do not intend to rush her and risk losing her forever."

"That is wise," their mother remarked, "but don't wait too long."

"I have no intention to."

Their mother nodded in approval. "I did come to remind you that Lady Langdon and Arabella will be joining us for dinner tonight."

"I am well aware," Colin said.

"Excellent," their mother responded. "We will also be playing games and lighting the Yule Log."

John interjected, "That is still a silly tradition."

"You two are no fun," their mother complained good-naturedly. "My brother and I used to fight about who was the first to sit on the log before it went into the fireplace."

"I promise that we will behave this evening," Colin assured her.

"That pleases me."

Colin walked over to his mother and kissed her on the cheek. "If you will excuse me, Arabella and I are going ice skating."

"That is promising," their mother acknowledged.

"It is, but I don't want to get ahead of myself," Colin said as he walked to the door. "I'm trying to win the war, not just the battle."

John smirked. "You should try to woo her with some of that war talk," he jested.

Colin shook his head. "Why am I cursed with a brother who is an idiot?"

"I feel the same way," John countered with a smile.

Colin departed from the library, excited to spend time with Arabella. She filled the empty pieces in his soul that he had desperately tried to pretend didn't exist. She was his heart, his other half.

Now he just had to convince her of that.

ARABELLA SAT in the drawing room with a book in her hand, but it was the furthest thing from her mind. Her head was filled with muddled thoughts of Colin. What was she going to do?

Why did she tell him that she still had feelings for him? That was a huge misstep on her part, considering she was unsure if she should even act on them. She had trusted Colin once, wholeheartedly, and he had betrayed her.

Her grandmother's voice broke through her musings. "You seem troubled, my dear."

"Do I?" she asked innocently.

"Did you even notice that your book is upside down?"

Arabella glanced down at the book and saw that it was right side up. "It is not."

"But you weren't sure, which leads me to believe you weren't focusing on it," her grandmother pointed out.

Arabella closed the book and placed it in her lap. "I'm afraid I was just thinking about Colin."

"I assumed as much."

"Why is he so maddening?"

Her grandmother smiled as she pulled a needle through the fabric. "I'm afraid I cannot answer that question."

"I was doing perfectly well without him."

"Were you?"

Arabella ran her finger over the edge of the book. "I wasn't doing terrible."

A Tangled Wreath

Her grandmother lowered her needlework. "Perhaps there is a reason Colin came back into your life."

"For what purpose? To aggravate me?"

"You two appeared to be getting along quite nicely yesterday when we were decorating the trees," her grandmother observed with a laugh.

"We were."

"Do you not owe it to yourself to give this relationship another try?"

Arabella sighed. "I don't rightly know."

"Why not?"

"I'm scared," she admitted softly. "What if Colin hurts me again?"

Her grandma gave her a compassionate look. "There is always that risk when dealing with matters of the heart."

Arabella lowered her gaze to her lap. "Frankly, I don't think I am strong enough."

"That is rubbish," her grandmother declared. "You are a strong, vibrant young woman."

"Not when it comes to Colin. I have always had a weak spot for him."

Their conversation came to an abrupt halt when Moore stepped into the room and met Arabella's gaze. "Lord Barrett has come to call," he informed her. "Would you care for me to show him in?"

"Yes, please," Arabella replied as she smoothed down her pink gown.

It was only a moment before Colin stepped into the room, simply but elegantly dressed in a blue riding jacket, buff trousers, and white cravat.

He stopped near the door and bowed. "Good afternoon, ladies."

"Would you care to sit and have some tea?" her grandmother asked, gesturing towards an upholstered armchair.

"I believe I shall," Colin replied.

After he was situated, Arabella's grandmother gave her a pointed look. "Would you care to pour the tea, Arabella?"

"It would be my pleasure." She moved to the edge of her seat and picked up the teapot on the tray. After she poured a cup, she extended it towards Colin.

"Thank you," he said as their fingers brushed up against one another, a tremor running up her arm.

Arabella leaned back, pretending his touch hadn't affected her. "How is your family?"

"They are well," Colin replied. "In fact, my brother is engaged."

"John is engaged?" Arabella repeated.

Colin smirked. "Didn't I just say that?" he asked.

"You did, but I'm afraid you have taken me by surprise," Arabella said. "I hadn't even realized he was courting anyone."

"Apparently, the engagement was rather sudden," Colin remarked.

Arabella nodded her understanding. "Is John happy, though?"

"He is," Colin said. "He was fortunate enough to discover that Lady Marjorie shares his affection."

Her grandmother spoke up. "That is good."

Colin took a long sip of tea before setting his cup down onto the tray. "Are you ready to go ice skating?"

"I am," Arabella replied.

He rose and offered his hand. "Allow me."

"Thank you," she replied as she allowed him to help her stand.

Colin took her hand and moved it to the crook of his arm. "My carriage is out front," he informed her.

"Splendid," she murmured.

As they walked into the entry hall, Moore extended

A Tangled Wreath

Arabella's pelisse and asked, "Would you care for a blanket, as well?"

"That won't be necessary," Colin responded. "I have blankets in the carriage for Lady Arabella."

Moore tipped his head. "Very good, milord."

As Colin escorted her outside, Arabella saw Peter running towards her with a wide smile on his face. He came to a stop in front of her, his breathing labored. "I was just hired to muck the stalls," he announced proudly.

"That is wonderful news," she declared.

Peter puffed out his chest proudly. "Thomas made me prove I could lift heavy objects around the stable, and he said that I was the strongest boy he has ever seen."

"You must be rather strong, then."

"I am," Peter said.

Arabella gestured towards Colin. "Peter, allow me to introduce you to Lord Barrett."

Peter's eyes grew panicked. "You are Lord Barrett?"

"I am."

"I… uh… should be getting back to the stables," Peter stammered out as he backed up. "I just wanted to thank you for the job."

"I only asked Thomas to meet with you," Arabella said. "You were the one who convinced him to hire you."

Peter mumbled his goodbyes before he spun on his heel and ran back towards the stable.

"That was odd," Colin commented.

Arabella nodded. "I would agree," she replied. "He was most likely nervous meeting you for the first time."

"Why would that be?"

"It could be the grimace that is on your lips," Arabella said.

"I do not grimace."

Arabella gave him a look. "You do," she replied. "You can come across as unapproachable."

"That is a good thing."

"Not to everyone."

Colin assisted her into the carriage. "I don't have time to solve people's trivial matters," he said. "I have an estate to run."

"That is precisely what I am talking about," Arabella responded as she situated herself on the bench. "Who are you to decide something is trivial?"

"A neighbor stealing laundry off the line is trivial," Colin said as he sat next to her.

"Not to the person who is out an article of clothing."

"That is why I employ a steward," he remarked. "He handles all the petty offenses."

Arabella shook her head. "I do not presume to know how to run an estate—"

He cut her off. "Yet you are going to advise me on how to do so," he teased. "Am I right?"

"You are," she said with a bob of her head. "I just think it is in your best interest to become invested in your tenant's lives."

"That would be a waste of my time."

"All right," she responded. "Forget I said anything."

Colin eyed her curiously. "What game are you playing, woman?"

She laughed. "I can assure you that I am not playing any game," she said. "I just know when to stop pestering you."

"Since when?"

"I don't want to ruin this lovely outing by arguing."

"That is the first logical thing you have said in a long time," Colin said, mirth in his eyes. "Are you feeling well?"

"I assure you that I am."

Colin smiled. "I must admit it is quite fun to win an argument against you."

"You didn't win," she pointed out. "I merely made the conscious decision not to argue back."

A Tangled Wreath

"Thus, I won," he remarked smugly.

"You are quite vexing," she said good-naturedly.

"So I have been told."

Arabella's lips twitched as she glanced over at Colin. She missed the friendship that once had existed between them. Frankly, she missed him, dearly.

Chapter Thirteen

Colin glanced over at Arabella as they rode in the carriage. He didn't think it was possible, but she had managed to grow more beautiful over the years. He noticed her cheeks were pink from the cold air and he asked, "Are you warm enough?"

"I am," she replied.

"Good. I would hate for you to catch cold."

"That is thoughtful of you."

A silence descended over them as Arabella's gaze left his and roamed the countryside. Before it grew awkward, he asked, "How do you know Peter?"

Arabella visibly tensed. "I met him in the village."

"Is he an orphan?"

"No, he has a mother," she replied. "She works in the milliner's shop."

Curious, he asked, "How did you come to help him find work in the stables?"

"He told me that he was looking for work, but no one was willing to hire him."

"Why do you suppose that was?"

"I assumed it was because of his age."

"But you aren't sure?"

Arabella frowned. "Why do I feel as if you are interrogating me?"

"I am doing no such thing," he replied. "I am just trying to make sense of how you know Peter."

Shifting on the bench, she turned to face him. "My grandmother and I went shopping in the village and Peter darted out in front of our coach," she explained. "Our driver started yelling at him and I stepped in to help console him."

"That was kind of you."

"It was the least I could do," she said. "After we spoke for a few moments, I gave him some money to go purchase some bread for me."

"Was it truly for you?"

"No, it was always for Peter," she remarked. "Once he returned with the bread, I claimed I wasn't hungry and offered it to him."

"How did you know he wouldn't take your money and run?"

"It was a chance I was willing to take, but I had a good feeling about him."

Colin nodded in approval. "You have a good heart, Bella."

"You would have done the same thing."

"I am not sure if that is true," Colin said. "You are much more observant when it comes to lending aid to others. It has always been that way."

A black coach became visible in the distance and their carriage moved to the side of the road so it could pass. As it did so, Arabella gasped.

"What's wrong?" Colin asked.

Arabella turned to watch the coach continue down the road. "That is Lord Eastwood's coach."

"How can you be sure?"

"It had his crest." She turned back around with a sigh. "Why in the blazes is he here?"

Colin chuckled. "Language, dear."

A Tangled Wreath

"I do apologize, but I informed him in a letter that I had no intention of marrying him."

"Then why is he here?"

"I know not, but I should probably go find out," she said.

"Would it be possible to go ice skating another time?"

"Of course," Colin replied, instructing the driver to turn the carriage around.

"I do apologize for this."

"You have no reason to apologize," he said. "You had no way of knowing that Lord Eastwood would come to call."

"I must admit that I was looking forward to going ice skating with you."

"Do not fret," he responded. "We shall try for another day."

"I hope so."

They rode in silence as they traveled the short distance back to the manor. Arabella was deep in thought, and Colin didn't dare try to interrupt her reverie.

They arrived in the courtyard and Colin exited the carriage, then turned and assisted Arabella out.

Arabella remained rooted in place as she stared up at the manor, and a line between her brows appeared.

"Whatever is the matter?"

"I hate confrontations," she admitted. "I find them to be uncomfortable and quite awkward."

"Why do you assume Lord Eastwood is here to confront you?"

"Why else would he be here?"

"Could he be bringing you a gift for Christmas?"

She gave him an exasperated look. "Do be serious."

Taking a step closer to her, Colin asked, "Would you care for me to remain with you?"

"Do you mind?"

He shook his head. "I do not," he replied. "It would be my pleasure."

"Thank you," she murmured.

He reached for her hand and gently squeezed it. "Shall we get this over with?"

"That would be wise," she replied, remaining still.

Taking her hand, he placed it in the crook of his arm. "Would you like me to carry you inside?"

Arabella gave him a baffled look. "Why would you ask such a thing?"

"Because you haven't moved from that spot."

"Good point," she muttered.

Colin took a step, encouraging her forward. "You need not fear," he said. "I won't let anything happen to you."

Her face softened. "Thank you."

"You don't have to keep thanking me," he said.

"I feel as if I must."

The door to the manor was held open by the butler and they stepped inside. After Moore closed the door, he said, "Lord Eastwood has come to call on you. He is being received by Lady Langdon."

"Thank you," Arabella said.

Colin led her towards the drawing room and stopped just outside of the door. "Are you ready to face him?"

She squared her shoulders and met his gaze. "I am."

"Then let us proceed," he said, leading her into the room.

Lady Langdon was sitting across from Lord Eastwood, and her eyes lit up when she saw them. "There you are, Arabella," she said. "I was just explaining to Lord Eastwood that you had just left to go ice skating with your dear friend, Lord Barrett."

Lord Eastwood rose and bowed. "It is lovely to see you again, Lady Arabella."

Arabella removed her hand from Colin's arm and curtsied. "I must admit I am rather surprised to see you," she said. "Did you not get my note?"

Lord Eastwood clenched his jaw. "Yes, I received it, but I

A Tangled Wreath

was hoping to speak to you about it." He hesitated. "Privately, if you don't mind."

Arabella considered him for a long moment before saying, "As you wish."

Rising, Lady Langdon said, "Lord Barrett and I will remain close by."

Colin leaned closer to Arabella and lowered his voice. "Are you sure you want to be alone with him?"

"I feel as if I must," she whispered back.

Lady Langdon walked over to the door and gave Colin an expectant look. "Are you coming, Lord Barrett?"

"I am." Colin turned back towards Arabella. "If you need me for any reason, I will be just on the other side of this door."

Arabella nodded her understanding, but her eyes remained fixated on Lord Eastwood.

As he walked over to the door, Colin noticed that Lord Eastwood was eyeing him with contempt. He followed Lady Langdon into the entry hall and asked, "Do you think leaving them alone is the best recourse?"

"I do," Lady Langdon said, spinning back around. "I believe it is in Arabella's best interest to have closure with Lord Eastwood."

"But to leave them alone?"

Lady Langdon waved her hand dismissively in front of her. "Do not be so prudish," she said. "We shall remain in the entry hall to ensure she isn't absconded."

He furrowed his brow. "Do you think he would do such a thing?"

She laughed. "Dear heavens, you are tightly wound today, my lord."

"I just do not like her conversing with that man," he said.

Lady Langdon gave him an understanding look. "You must trust her, in all things," she counseled.

"I do, but..." His voice trailed off as he attempted to

find the right words. He couldn't help but wonder if Arabella might change her mind about marrying Lord Eastwood.

Lady Langdon smiled. "Trust her," she urged.

Colin sighed. "I do."

Gesturing towards two chairs in the entry hall, Lady Langdon asked, "Would you care to sit?"

"I would."

After they were situated, Colin's eyes remained focused on the drawing room door. He knew he was behaving like a jealous suitor, but there was so much at stake. He wanted Arabella for his wife. She may not need him, but he needed her, desperately.

AFTER COLIN and her grandmother departed from the room, Arabella gave Lord Eastwood an expectant look. She didn't quite know what to say to him. He was a handsome man, and she was well aware that he had always used that to his advantage. But she would not fall for his charming act again.

Lord Eastwood smiled, no doubt trying to disarm her. "Arabella," he said. "How have you been faring?"

"Not well."

"Why is that?" he asked.

She shook her head. "I suppose it has something to do with my fiancé running off to Gretna Green with another woman."

Lord Eastwood frowned. "I can explain."

"You can?" she asked. "Because I can't quite understand why you would offer for me but choose to elope with Lady Georgiana instead."

"It is complicated."

"Then *un*complicate it," she remarked dryly.

A Tangled Wreath

Lord Eastwood gestured towards the settee. "Would you care to sit and speak about this rationally?"

"I suppose I can agree to that." She walked over and lowered herself onto the settee. "I do find myself curious as to why you traveled all the way here."

Lord Eastwood sat down and shifted to face her. "As I mentioned in my note, my father is adamant that you and I should wed."

"Did he give a reason?"

"He wishes to unite our families through marriage."

Arabella clasped her hands in her lap. "You must understand that I couldn't possibly marry you now, given the circumstances."

"I made a trivial mistake..."

She spoke over him. "A trivial mistake?" she repeated in disbelief. "Is that what you call it?"

"Lady Georgiana and I have always had a special bond, but I assure you that I will be more discreet moving forward," Lord Eastwood remarked.

Her mouth dropped. "Am I to understand that you would continue to carry on with her once we were married?"

Lord Eastwood shifted uncomfortably in his seat. "It is not uncommon for a man of my station to have a mistress."

"You are unbelievable," she said with a shake of her head.

"If you would prefer, I would be willing to wait a few months before I pursue Lady Georgiana again," he offered.

Arabella abruptly rose. "I think you should go."

"But we haven't decided anything yet."

"I have made my decision," she stated. "I will not now, not ever, marry you."

Jumping to his feet, he replied, "But we must!"

"Why is that?" she asked, crossing her arms over her chest.

He winced slightly. "If we don't wed, then my father won't give me my allowance," he admitted. "I will be penniless."

"I don't believe that to be true."

Lord Eastwood put a hand on her arm. "Furthermore, if you don't marry me, then you will become a spinster."

"That is not a certainty."

He lifted his brow. "You have had two broken engagements," he reminded her. "No sensible man will look at you twice."

"I understand, but I do believe that being a spinster is a better alternative than marrying you."

Lord Eastwood gave her a blank stare. "You don't mean that."

"I do," she replied, tilting her chin.

"Now you are just being unreasonable," he said.

"I'm being unreasonable?" she repeated, her voice rising. "You are the one who eloped with another woman!"

"And I apologized for that," he said. "Can we not move forward?"

"No, we can't!"

Lord Eastwood walked over to the fireplace and put his hands on the mantle, leaning in. "Your father led me to believe that you would be much more agreeable."

"I do apologize that you have been forced to travel all this way on Christmas Eve, but my mind is made up."

"You would rather be a drain on your family's household than marry me?" he asked in disbelief. "I will be a marquess one day."

"I am well aware of your status."

With a huff, he said, "You are being incredibly selfish, Arabella."

"How so?"

"Your father went to great lengths to ensure that we were wed," Lord Eastwood said, pushing off the mantle.

"Regardless, you are the one who broke this engagement by doing something utterly terrible."

Tossing his hands up in the air, Lord Eastwood exclaimed, "How many times do I have to apologize to you?"

"It will never be enough for me to change my mind."

Lord Eastwood narrowed his eyes. "You knew what I was like when you accepted my offer of marriage," he said. "What has changed?"

"It matters not."

"It most assuredly does matter," Lord Eastwood declared. "This is my future we are talking about."

Her eyes darted towards the door, but she remained quiet.

Lord Eastwood followed her gaze. "Do you truly believe that Lord Barrett will want you, considering he rejected you once already?" he asked haughtily.

"Lord Barrett and I are just friends."

"I do not believe that," he argued, shaking his head. "I can see in your eyes that you have hope for him."

"That has nothing to do with us."

Lord Eastwood walked over, stopping in front of her. "I do not have an issue with sharing you, if that is your concern."

She reared back. "You are a scoundrel."

"I have been called worse."

"I think it is time for you to go," she said, holding his gaze unflinchingly.

"You will regret this," Lord Eastwood warned.

"No, I don't believe I will," she stated firmly.

Lord Eastwood stared at her for a moment before heading towards the door. He stopped and spun back around. "Let me know if you change your mind."

"I don't anticipate it, my lord."

"You are an insufferable woman," he said. "I doubt we would have suited."

"For once, we do agree on something."

Lord Eastwood departed from the room, and it was only a moment before she heard the main door slam shut.

Colin appeared in the doorway. "I take it that didn't go well."

"No, it did not."

He stepped forward into the room. "Would you care to talk about it?"

"I do, but not at this time."

"I understand," he replied. "Take all the time that you need."

Arabella approached and gave him a weak smile. "Thank you for understanding."

To her surprise, he leaned in and kissed her forehead. "Go rest up for dinner," he encouraged, leaning back. "I can't have you falling asleep when you dine with us this evening."

"A nap sounds heavenly," she sighed.

As she departed from the drawing room, she reached up to touch where his lips had met her forehead. That had been completely unexpected, and completely wonderful.

Chapter Fourteen

Colin sat alone in his study as he read through a pile of correspondence. It was a never-ending task that he dreaded, but it had to be done. He would much rather spend time with Arabella, especially since she was the only bright spot in his gloomy world. For him, she was perfect.

As he reached for another letter, he saw it was from the investigator he'd hired to make inquiries about Sam Burkard. He eagerly unfolded the letter and read the contents.

John stepped into the study. "You look troubled," he commented.

"I'm afraid I am."

"Why is that?"

Colin dropped the letter to his desk. "It would appear that Sam Burkard was raised in the neighboring village of Langham," he said. "But that is all the investigator could discover about him."

"That's not much."

"Apparently, some documents from the army were destroyed when a roof leaked," Colin explained.

"That is most unfortunate."

"It is," he agreed. "The investigator requests permission to travel to Langham to find additional information."

His brother eyed him with concern. "Then what?"

"I will do right by Sam."

"But he is dead."

"Don't you think I know that?" Colin asked gruffly. "He gave his life for mine, and I intend to ensure it was not in vain."

John walked over to the chair in front of the desk and sat down. "You don't need to feel guilty about being alive."

"But I do," Colin replied, "every single day."

"You must let that go."

"How do you propose I do that?"

John gave him an apologetic shrug. "I don't rightly know."

Colin pushed back his chair and walked over to the drink cart. He picked up the decanter and poured two glasses. As he walked one over to his brother, he said, "I should have never survived the war."

"But you did," John responded, accepting the glass.

Colin brought his own up to his lips. "How is it fair that I did when so many good men died?"

"You must look at it differently."

"How so?"

John placed his glass onto the desk. "You were fortunate enough to make it out alive and now you have the rest of your life to do good."

Colin scoffed. "You sound like Arabella."

"She isn't wrong."

Colin tightened his hold around his glass. "I don't think I will be able to move on until I know that Sam's family is provided for," he said. "It is the least I can do."

"I don't fault you for that."

After he took a sip of his drink, Colin admitted, "I knew so little about him."

A Tangled Wreath

"I imagine you don't have a lot of time to chit chat when you're fighting in a war," John remarked.

"That's true, but I wish I had spent more time getting to know him."

Before his brother could respond, his mother glided into the room and announced, "Lady Langdon and Arabella will be here shortly."

"Wonderful," Colin muttered.

His mother glanced between them. "Why the gloomy faces?" she asked. "It's Christmas Eve!"

Colin returned his glass to the drink cart. "I'm afraid I am not in the Christmas spirit this evening."

"You will be once Arabella shows up," his mother remarked knowingly. "I even had mistletoe hung over the doorway in the drawing room. With any luck, you may get to kiss her tonight."

A smile came to his lips at that thought. "I wouldn't be opposed to that."

"Of course not, dear," his mother said. "I wish I could follow you around with mistletoe, but Arabella might not appreciate that."

He chuckled. "No, I don't imagine that she would."

"Shall we adjourn to the drawing room?" his mother suggested.

John rose and tugged down on his maroon waistcoat. "I do wish Marjorie was spending Christmas with us."

"As do I," their mother said.

They had barely arrived at the drawing room's threshold when a knock came at the main door. A thrill of excitement shot through Colin at the thought of seeing Arabella again.

Dickson opened the door, revealing Arabella and Lady Langdon. They stepped inside and removed their coats. Colin took a moment to admire Arabella, noting she looked the vision of perfection. Her hair was piled high atop her head and small curls framed her face. She was dressed in a lovely jonquil gown, highlighting her comely figure.

Arabella glanced over at him and a bright smile lit her face. "Why are you loitering outside the drawing room?"

"I don't think I can loiter in my own home."

"You make a valid point," she replied, closing the distance between them. "Were you waiting for us?"

"I will always wait for you, Bella," he murmured.

A blush came to her cheeks at his words. "You are being rather charming tonight."

"Aren't I always?"

"No, at times you can be downright boorish," she said, her words light.

He grinned. "Aren't you supposed to be nice to people on Christmas Eve?"

"I apologize, my lord," she replied, amusement in her voice.

Colin turned his attention towards Lady Langdon and bowed. "Good evening," he greeted. "How are you this evening?"

"I am well," Lady Langdon said. "Is your mother in the drawing room?"

"She is," he confirmed.

"If you will excuse me, I shall go speak to her," she responded.

After Lady Langdon stepped into the drawing room, Colin took a step closer to Arabella. "How are you faring?" he asked, his voice low. "And I would prefer the truth, if you don't mind."

"Why do you assume I would lie to you?" Arabella asked.

"You always say you are fine, but I can see the pain lurking in your eyes."

"I could say the same thing about you," Arabella said.

Colin's eyes searched hers. "I have no doubt, but you have managed to ease my suffering tremendously."

"In what way?"

"Just knowing I can see you, speak to you, has caused me to find hope again."

Arabella lowered her gaze as she admitted, "I must admit that I have found some solace in you, as well."

"I am pleased to hear that." The sound of his mother laughing in the drawing room drew his attention. "We should probably join the festivities."

"That sounds like a fine idea."

As she moved to brush by him, Colin placed his hand on her sleeve. "Would you care to go riding tomorrow morning?"

"On Christmas?"

Colin nodded. "I understand if you don't want to…"

"I would love to."

"Then I shall see you tomorrow."

Arabella gave him an amused look. "We still have tonight to get through."

He leaned closer to her and murmured, "Every moment I spend with you is a moment I treasure."

A pretty blush stained her cheeks. "You are being very complimentary this evening."

"It is merely the truth, Bella," he said as he leaned back.

Arabella opened her mouth to speak but closed it before saying anything. He waited a moment, not wanting to rush her.

Finally, she spoke, her words soft. "We should join the others."

Colin found himself disappointed by her lack of response, but he quickly brought a smile to his face. "After you, my lady."

He watched her walk into the drawing room and sighed. He would find a way to break through her defenses, one by one.

ARABELLA WOKE to the sounds of a fire crackling in the hearth. She sat up in bed and felt a smile growing on her face. Not only was today Christmas, but she was also going riding with Colin. No matter how much she tried to deny her feelings for him, she knew she was failing horribly. Frankly, she wasn't sure if she wanted to anymore.

It was exhausting to try to ignore the stirrings in her heart, especially since a part of her had always loved him. However, she had to be certain that he wouldn't hurt her again. His words may be full of love and whatnot, but she had been fooled before.

A knock came at her door, breaking her out of her musings.

"Enter," she ordered.

The door opened, and her lady's maid stepped into the room. "I was just informed that Lord Barrett has arrived and is waiting for you downstairs."

Arabella threw off her covers and put her feet over the side of the bed. "We should hurry, then."

"My sentiments exactly," Mary said.

Rising, Arabella went and sat at the dressing table. Mary picked up the brush and started brushing her long tresses.

"Do you have anything planned for Christmas?" Arabella asked.

Mary put the brush down and picked up some pins. "I do not, but I understand the cook is preparing a delicious spread for us."

"Again, I am sorry that you are missing Christmas with your family," Arabella said.

With a shrug, Mary admitted, "My siblings were committed to work on Christmas anyways."

"I am sorry to hear that."

"We will celebrate later," Mary said as she pinned back her hair. "We usually get together for dinner as a family and exchange gifts that we have made for one another."

A Tangled Wreath

"That sounds lovely."

A short time later, Arabella emerged from her room dressed in her dark green riding habit. She hurried down the hall, finding herself eager to see Colin. She had just started descending the stairs when she saw him standing in the entry hall. He was dressed in a grey riding jacket, dark trousers, and black Hessian boots.

Colin turned his head and met her gaze. "Good morning," he greeted.

"I hope I did not keep you waiting for too long," she responded as she came to stand in front of him.

"You did not," he said. "Besides, it was entirely my fault, since I arrived earlier than I had intended."

"Why is that?"

He smiled, a dashing smile that caused a fluttering in her stomach. "Do you even need to ask?"

Arabella fought the blush that she felt forming on her cheeks. Rather than answer his question, she asked one of her own. "Are you ready to go?"

"I am." Colin gestured towards the door. "I took the liberty of asking Moore to see to your horse being saddled."

"That was thoughtful of you."

Once they stepped outside, Colin walked over to the left side of Arabella's horse and said, "Allow me." He intertwined his fingers and leaned down.

"Thank you," she murmured as she placed her hands on his shoulders and allowed him to assist her onto her side saddle.

Once she was situated, she reached for the reins from the groom and waited for Colin to mount.

"Where should we ride to?" Colin asked.

"Follow me," she said, kicking her horse into a run.

Arabella felt the wind on her face as she leaned lower in her saddle. She glanced over and was pleased to see Colin riding next to her. As she turned towards the woodlands,

Colin slowed his horse's gait and trailed behind her on the path.

They arrived at the stream, and she reined in her horse. "I thought today would be a brilliant day to visit the stream."

Colin gave her a knowing smile. "I should just gift you this parcel of land."

"I would greatly appreciate that," she replied cheekily. "It would save me the trouble of having to trespass on your land."

"You are always welcome on my lands, Bella."

After Arabella effortlessly dismounted, she saw an iron bench sitting a few yards back from the stream. "Where did this bench come from?"

Colin smiled. "I had it brought down here for you," he said. "I thought it would be much more comfortable than sitting on a fallen log."

"That was very thoughtful of you," she acknowledged.

He shrugged off her praise. "It was a small thing."

Arabella walked over to the bench and sat down. She leaned her head back and looked up at the trees. "It is so lovely here," she said. "I could stay in this spot forever."

"You would starve if you did so," Colin joked.

"But I would die happy."

Colin walked over to the bench and pointed to the seat next to her. "May I?"

"Please," she encouraged.

After he sat down, he asked, "Now, will you tell me what transpired between you and Lord Eastwood that caused you to be so upset?"

She huffed. "Lord Eastwood is insufferable."

"I will not disagree with you there," Colin said. "He has always been too cocky for his own good, even when we were at Eton."

"Lord Eastwood was adamant that we should be wed at once."

"Why?"

A Tangled Wreath

"He claims that his father will cut his allowance if he fails to do so."

"But you don't believe him?"

"I am unsure," she replied. "Frankly, I don't trust anything that comes out of Lord Eastwood's mouth."

"That is wise."

Frowning, Arabella shared, "Furthermore, he assured me that once we were married, he would be more discreet when pursuing Lady Georgiana."

Colin's brow lifted. "He said that?"

"He did."

"Idiot," Colin muttered. "I apologize that he said something so crass to you."

"It is not your fault," she responded. "I knew he was a rake, but I was fortunate enough to have learned the full extent before I was shackled to him."

The sound of a gunshot could be heard in the distance. Arabella turned to Colin and saw that his face had paled.

"Are you all right?" she asked.

"I will be," he said, his breathing strained.

She shifted on the bench to face him. "How can I help you?"

"Nothing can be done," he asserted, looking at the ground. "It will pass in due time."

Unsure of what to do, she simply put a hand on his sleeve and murmured, "It will be all right."

Eventually, his breathing returned to normal. He looked up at her sheepishly. "I do apologize about that."

"What happened?"

"The gun discharging suddenly brought me back to the war, and I panicked." He grimaced. "I wish you hadn't witnessed that."

"Why not?"

"You must think me a broken man."

She shook her head. "I thought no such thing."

Colin jumped up from his seat. "How can you not?" he asked. "I am broken."

"You most assuredly are not," she responded firmly.

"A sane man would not react in such a fashion to a gun discharging," he said, looking down upon her.

Rising, Arabella maintained his gaze. "What I see is a man who is struggling with his past," she said.

His eyes became sad. "I wish these overwhelming feelings of panic would go away."

"They will."

"How can you be so sure?" he asked softly.

"Because I will find a way to help you."

She saw his eyes become moist with tears, something she never thought she would witness. "No one can help me," he whispered.

The pain in his voice was her undoing, and she reached out and cupped his cheek. "You are the bravest man I know," she said firmly. "You fought for your country; now let me fight for you."

Colin nodded solemnly. "All right."

"Good," she said, removing her hand. "I'm glad that you can be reasonable about it."

He let out a slight chuckle. "You can be quite convincing, my dear."

Glancing over at her horse, Arabella said, "I should be heading back. I promised my grandmother that I would go to church with her this morning."

"Then we should get back."

Chapter Fifteen

With the morning sun streaming into the windows, Colin sat at his desk attempting to get some work done. His eyes may have been on the ledgers, but his mind was dwelling on Arabella.

He couldn't believe how collected she had been when he'd had one of his episodes yesterday. She had remained by his side, offering encouragement in a soothing voice. How could he not love this woman? Arabella was the reason he smiled first thing in the morning, and the thought of her put him to sleep every night. He could see her softening towards him, and he hoped she would come to realize that they belonged together.

A knock came at the door, and his gamekeeper stepped into the room. "You wished to see me, milord?"

"I did," Colin said, closing the ledger. "I do apologize for disturbing you on your day off, but something disturbing happened the other day."

Burton walked further into the room. "Which was?"

"A gunshot in the woodlands yesterday morning," Colin shared. "By chance, were you or your men hunting in the woods?"

"We were not," Burton replied, looking displeased. "It must have been the poacher we are tracking."

Colin leaned back in his chair. "That is rather upsetting." "My men and I are doing everything in our power to find this criminal, but your woodlands are quite extensive."

"Perhaps I could help."

Burton shook his head. "It is much too dangerous," he argued. "Poachers can turn violent when confronted."

"I understand the risks, but I am tired of someone stealing from me in such a brazen fashion," Colin asserted.

"I assure you that we are doing all we can, and we will eventually catch this person," Burton remarked. "The constable is still on the case, as well."

"Does he have any leads?"

"Not at this time."

Colin frowned. "How has this poacher managed to elude us for so long?"

"I know not, but I do not intend to rest until this man is in jail."

"I do appreciate that."

Burton tipped his head. "Will there be anything else?"

"Not at this time," Colin replied.

After Burton left the room, Colin rose from his chair and walked over to the window. This poacher may be crafty, but he would find a way to catch him.

His brother's voice came from the doorway. "I know that look," John said. "You are plotting something."

Colin turned towards his brother and replied, "I'm thinking about how I intend to stop the poacher who has continued to elude my men."

"Most likely, he is just someone from the village trying to earn some money to feed his family," John said.

"That may be true, but he is still stealing from me." Colin's words came out much harsher than he had intended.

A Tangled Wreath

"I agree," John said, putting his hands up. "I was merely offering my thoughts on the matter."

Colin sighed. "I do apologize. I had no reason to lash out at you."

"Consider it forgotten."

"Thank you." Colin eyed his brother curiously. "May I ask why you are up so early?"

"I have come to say my goodbyes."

"You have?"

"I am returning to London until my wedding," John shared. "I have no doubt that my caseload has increased tenfold since I left."

"Have you informed Mother of your decision?"

"I have," John replied. "I have only just come from her bedchamber."

"Then I wish you Godspeed on your trip."

John watched him for a moment, then said, "And I wish you luck with Arabella."

"I appreciate that, but I do believe she is softening towards me."

"I am relieved to know that, especially since you are much more tolerable with her around," John teased.

Colin chuckled. "I don't disagree with you there."

John grew serious. "Just don't give up on her," he said. "She is a woman worth fighting for."

"I should never have let her go," Colin remarked.

"No, you shouldn't have."

"At the time, I thought I was doing the right thing," Colin said dejectedly.

"Fate has been kind to you and given you a second chance with her."

Colin nodded. "I agree," he replied. "I have been most fortunate."

"I do hope to be attending your wedding soon enough."

"With any luck, it will be shortly after your wedding with Lady Marjorie."

John smiled ruefully. "Just not too soon," he joked. "I do intend to have a proper wedding tour."

Colin could see the happiness etched on his brother's face. "I am happy for you."

"Thank you," John responded. "But this is not a true goodbye, since I shall see you at my wedding."

"I wouldn't miss it."

"I am hoping that you will stand up with me when I am wed."

Colin tipped his head. "I would be honored to."

"Wonderful," John said, walking over to the door. "I shall see you soon."

After his brother departed from the study, it only took a moment for Colin to decide that he wanted to go in search of this allusive poacher. He located his butler and ordered his horse to be brought around front.

As he waited in the entry hall, he saw his mother descending the stairs, dressed in a maroon gown. She came to a stop in front of him and asked, "Will you be joining me for breakfast this morning?"

"I will not."

"Why is that?"

"I intend to go searching for the poacher who is plaguing my lands."

His mother gave him a disapproving look. "Do you think that is wise?"

"I can hardly be expected to sit back and do nothing while someone robs me of my game," Colin asserted.

"You have a gamekeeper to handle these sorts of situations."

"I agree, but he has failed in that regard."

"You are an earl now and you mustn't take unnecessary risks."

A Tangled Wreath

Colin leaned forward and kissed her on the cheek. "You need not worry about me, Mother."

"I will always worry about you," she replied. "That is the job of any good mother."

"I served in the army, and I daresay that Napoleon's forces are more worrisome than a lone poacher."

His mother didn't appear convinced by his words. "I have heard about the terrible practices poachers employ to avoid capture," she said. "Promise me that you will try to use some caution."

"I can promise you that."

"I have already lost one son, and I don't intend to lose another."

Colin gave her a reassuring smile. "What you've heard is probably about gangs of poachers raiding an area, killing all the game," he stated. "That is not what is happening here."

"I shall have to trust you, then." She paused. "Although, you could always take a groom along with you."

"That won't be necessary," he said.

The butler stepped back into the entry hall and announced, "Your horse has been saddled and is waiting out front."

Colin turned back towards his mother. "May I leave now?"

"You may," she replied with a wave of her hand. "Be off with you, before I change my mind."

"Thank you, Mother," he said before departing the manor.

ARABELLA RACED her horse across the fields and enjoyed the cold, crisp air on her face. She'd had a restless night, and she needed to clear her mind. There had to be a way to help Colin overcome these episodes of overwhelming panic, but she was at a loss. The thought of Colin having any pain caused her heart to ache.

Up ahead, she saw Colin duck his horse into the woodlands and decided to see what he was about. She leaned lower in the saddle until she arrived where she saw him disappear.

Slowing her horse's gait, she proceeded onto the well-worn path. The tree coverage grew denser, and she saw no sign of Colin. She was just about to give up when she heard a horse whinnying in the distance.

Arabella urged her mount forward, leaving the safety of the path behind. It wasn't long before she saw Colin's horse, but she saw no sign of him.

"Drat," she muttered under her breath.

Knowing that her horse needed a break, she dismounted and walked over to Colin's horse. "Where is your master?" she asked as she rubbed the horse's neck.

Colin's voice came from behind her. "It isn't wise for you to be this far into the woodlands."

Turning back to face him, she said, "I came in search of you."

"In here?"

She shrugged one shoulder. "You might say that I was bored."

He looked amused. "I daresay that you need a new pastime, then."

"My grandmother would be pleased if I practiced my needlework more, but I find it to be dreadfully boring."

"I am not surprised."

Arabella took a moment to admire the dashing figure that Colin made. He was dressed in a dark green riding jacket, dark trousers, and a white cravat. His hair was brushed forward, and she had the strangest urge to run her hands through it.

To distract herself from her own thoughts, she asked, "May I ask why you are out here by yourself?"

A Tangled Wreath

"I am catching a poacher." He paused. "At least, I am trying to."

"Why do you say that?"

"I found a trap, but the poacher might not return to this spot if he sees us chatting out in the open," Colin said. "If you promise to be quiet, I will let you join me."

She smiled. "I promise."

Colin spun on his heel. "Follow me, then."

He led her a short distance away and crouched behind a cluster of birch trees. As she did the same, he whispered, "I noticed someone set a trap for small animals over there by the rocks."

"How do you know this person will show up to check the trap?"

"I don't," he replied.

She turned her attention towards the cluster of rocks. "May I ask how long you intend to stay out here?"

"All day, if I have to."

Arabella leaned closer to him and asked, "Don't you have servants to handle this sort of thing?"

"I do, but they have failed in this regard."

She turned her head back towards Colin and realized that their faces were only inches apart. "You have always been rather impatient," she said, her words sounding forced to her own ears.

"I won't disagree with you there." His eyes darted towards her lips, and she found herself hoping that he would kiss her.

She inhaled raggedly, her chest rising and falling with deep breaths as he moved closer. As his lips brushed against hers, she closed her eyes and melted into the kiss. His lips were warmer and softer than anything she could have imagined, but somehow they were fierce and powerful at the same time.

A twig breaking in the distance startled her, and she jumped back. She stared at Colin and was surprised to see him smiling back at her.

"If you want me to apologize, you will surely be disappointed," he said lightly.

"No, I don't want an apology."

"Good, because I am not sorry about kissing you." He brought his finger to his lips, indicating she should be quiet. As she turned her attention towards the rocks, she saw a familiar figure approach and her heart dropped. It was Peter.

Colin reached behind him and pulled out a pistol. Her eyes grew wide at the sight of it, and he whispered, "It is better to be safe than sorry."

Peter walked over to the trap and crouched down. As he tinkered with it, Colin rose and stepped out from behind the trees. "Stay where you are," he ordered.

Peter turned towards Colin with wide eyes, choosing to remain silent.

Colin approached him, his gun pointing at the boy. "Are you armed?"

With a shake of his head, Peter replied, "I'm not."

"I am going to put my pistol away, but you better not run," Colin directed before he tucked the pistol into the waistband of his trousers.

Peter rose and stood before Colin with a shaking frame. "I was just here to check my trap."

"I am well aware of what you were doing," Colin said. "Are you aware that poaching is a crime?"

Lowering his gaze, Peter replied, "Yes."

"Then why would you risk going to jail?"

"My mother and I were hungry."

Colin frowned as he glanced over his shoulder at Arabella. "Are you not employed at Lady Langdon's estate?"

"I am."

"Then why are you still poaching?"

Peter kicked at a rock on the ground. "I don't get my wages for another week," he said, "and my mother just got fired from her job."

"Why is that?"

"They accused her of having a child out of wedlock."

"Are you illegitimate?"

"No, milord," Peter responded, squaring his shoulders. "My father died in the war."

Arabella stepped closer to Colin as he asked, "How long ago did he die?"

"Four years," Peter responded.

Colin gave him a disapproving look. "Doesn't your mother have proof that the wedding took place?"

Peter shook his head. "There was a fire at our house, and it burned along with most of our things."

"It is not uncommon for women to pretend to be wed when they have a child outside the bands of matrimony," Colin said.

"My mother is not a whore!" Peter exclaimed. "She married my father, and he left to fight in the war."

"Have you never met your father?" Colin asked.

"I have met him," Peter replied. "I would see him when he came home on leave."

Arabella felt compassion swell inside of her for the boy. "Would it help if I saw to an advance of your wages?"

Colin turned to face her, his boots grinding on the loose rock. "How do you know he isn't lying?"

"Why would he lie about such a thing?" Arabella asked, keeping her voice low.

"To stay out of jail."

"I don't believe that to be the case." Arabella gestured towards the boy. "His cheeks are sunken in, and it looks like he hasn't had a good meal in a long time."

Colin considered her for a long moment, then said, "I will reserve judgment until I have spoken to his mother."

"Please, no!" Peter shouted frantically. "My mother doesn't know that I've been hunting on your land."

"Where does she believe the game is coming from?" Colin asked.

"She thinks I work at the inn."

"Why does she believe that?"

Peter pressed his lips into a straight line. "I told her that so I could explain why I had money to buy food."

"Are you selling the game you poach?" Colin pressed.

Peter nodded slowly. "To the innkeeper," he said.

"What precisely have you sold to him?"

"Mostly rabbits, squirrels and pheasants," Peter responded. "However, I did manage to kill a deer."

"How were you able to do so?"

"With my father's pistol," Peter said, sounding a bit proud. "I waited in the brush for hours until I saw a deer close enough that I could shoot."

Colin cocked his head. "Did you use that pistol on Christmas morning?"

"I did," Peter replied. "I made so much off the last deer that I hoped to get another one so I could buy my mother a present."

"You are stealing from me, and that cannot go unanswered," Colin said firmly. "It is time that we go speak to your mother."

Peter's eyes grew panicked. "I can work it off," he rushed out. "There must be another way."

"I'm afraid not," Colin said. "If I discover that you lied to me, then I will go straight to the magistrate."

Peter turned his pleading gaze towards her. "Please, Lady Arabella," he started, "I know I promised that I would stop poaching, but we can't afford to eat and pay our rent."

Colin looked at her in surprise. "You knew Peter was poaching on my lands and you didn't tell me?"

Arabella furrowed her brows. "I did, but only because I made him promise not to do it again."

"He lied to you," Colin stated. "Just as you lied to me."

A Tangled Wreath

She opened her mouth to argue, but she closed them when she knew there was no point. Colin was right. She had intentionally deceived him. "I'm sorry," she said. "That wasn't my intention."

"Then what was?" Colin asked.

"I felt bad for Peter's plight," Arabella said, "and I wanted to find a way to help him."

Colin's jaw tensed. "His supposed plight." He shifted his gaze to Peter. "Where do you live?"

"On the other side of these trees, just south of the village," Peter replied.

"You are one of my tenants?"

Peter nodded. "We are."

"Not for long," he muttered, gesturing towards the tree. "Show us the way to your home."

Chapter Sixteen

Colin trailed behind Arabella and Peter as they made their way to his home. He had every intention of making good on his promise to notify the constable if he discovered Peter had lied to him. He would not be made a fool of.

The thought that Arabella had intentionally deceived him did not sit well with him. Why hadn't she trusted him enough to come forward with this information? It made him wonder if he had made any progress with her. Although, they had kissed, and it had been a memorable moment for him. He had dreamt about that since he had first seen her again.

He watched as Arabella chatted with Peter, as if she didn't have a care in the world. She had a kind heart, and she always seemed to believe the best in people, but he would not be deceived so easily by a scrawny young man.

Peter glanced over his shoulder and said, "It is only a few more yards."

As they exited the cover of the trees, he saw a dilapidated cottage with a collapsing thatched roof. The windows were broken and stuffed with cloth. The main door was tilted, allowing the cold air to pass through the openings.

Colin came to an abrupt halt. "This is where you live?"

"It is," Peter said as he came to a stop in front of the door. "My mother should be inside."

Colin's eyes roamed the cottage, and he grew increasingly irritated. This place was uninhabitable, yet somehow he had tenants dwelling in it.

Arabella gave him a questioning gaze as she remained near the door. He hurried over to her and opened the door, following her inside.

The one-room structure was drafty, despite having a fire in the hearth. Two straw mattresses were pushed against the walls in the back, and the floorboards were deteriorating.

His eyes finally landed on a thin woman with a cap covering her dark hair. Her dress was clean but tattered. She stared at him with wide eyes for a moment, then she dipped a curtsy. "Milord," she murmured.

"How is it that you know who I am?" Colin asked.

She looked baffled. "Everyone knows who you are."

"I see." He gestured towards Arabella. "Allow me to introduce you to Lady Arabella."

The woman curtsied again. "It is an honor to have you in our home." Her eyes landed on the small, round table with a few pieces of bread. "The only thing I can offer you is bread, but I should warn you that it is a few days old."

Colin raised his hand. "Thank you for the kind offer, but I would prefer to get down to business."

"Is this because our rent is late?" the woman asked, her eyes growing fearful. "I told Mr. Brown that I was a few coins short, but I would get him the money."

"I am not here for that," Colin said.

Peter spoke up from next to his mother. "He is here because of what I did."

"I'm afraid I don't understand," the woman said, glancing between them.

Colin gave Peter an expectant look. "Would you like to confess, or should I tell your mother what you have done?"

Peter hesitated before admitting, "Lord Barrett caught me hunting on his land."

She gasped, her hands flying up to her mouth. "Tell me it isn't so."

"Did you know that he was poaching?" Colin asked.

With a shake of her head, she replied, "I did not, but we shall find a way to pay you back." She turned towards Peter. "Won't we, Peter?"

Peter nodded. "We will," he said.

"I was recently fired from the milliner's shop, but I am trying to find work," the woman shared.

Arabella interjected, "Peter informed us that you were fired because you couldn't find proof that you were married to your husband."

"That's true," the woman said. "My husband and I were married, and he left shortly thereafter to fight in the war."

"That must have been hard for you," Arabella acknowledged.

The woman smiled. "We didn't know I was increasing at the time, but he believed he would make his fortune in the army. Whenever he could, he sent back his wages to provide for us."

"Have you gone back to speak to the clergyman who married you?"

"Unfortunately, he died shortly after we were wed," the woman said. "He was quite old, and his heart gave out while he was giving a sermon."

"What about your witnesses?" Colin asked.

"I'm afraid we didn't know them," the woman admitted. "We paid a small fee to have two witnesses come in off the street."

"How did you come to lose the marriage lines?" Arabella questioned.

"One night it was particularly cold, and I put one too

many logs on the fire," the woman said. "We were lucky that we were able to escape with our lives."

"What of the parish clerk?" Arabella asked. "Have you asked to see the parish register book to prove that you were legally wed?"

"I have tried, but the clerk claims he has no record of our wedding."

"How is that possible?"

"I know not," the woman replied.

"Do you have no family or friends who could vouch for you?" Colin pressed.

The woman shook her head. "My husband grew up in a neighboring village, but he is the son of a migrant worker. He grew up sleeping on the streets and begging for food. No one glanced his way, much less learned his name."

"What of you?" Arabella asked.

"I was disowned by my parents when I agreed to marry Sam," the woman revealed. "My father owned the general store and I used to sneak food out to him. We struck up a friendship and fell in love."

"Surely someone could verify your union?" Colin questioned incredulously.

"I'm afraid not, milord," she replied. "Fate has not been kind to us, but I do swear to you that I was legally married before God and witnesses."

Arabella stepped forward and smiled. "I believe you."

The woman let out a sigh of relief. "That makes me so happy to hear," she said. "You have no idea how unkind people can be to me and my son."

Colin glanced around the cottage. "Have you informed Mr. Brown of all the repairs that need to be done to this cottage?"

"I do not wish to complain," the woman said. "We are lucky to have a roof over our heads."

"That doesn't make it right."

A Tangled Wreath

The woman gave him a sad smile. "It is still far better than our last home."

Colin blinked. "That is impossible."

"It had a dirt floor," Peter interjected, "and we shared it with animals."

Arabella turned her gaze towards Colin and gave him a look. They needed to help this family. If they didn't, they might not last through the winter.

"If it would help, I could speak to my solicitor and see if there was a way to prove you were legally wed," Colin offered.

The woman gave him an appreciative look. "That would be exceptionally kind of you, milord."

"You mentioned you came from a neighboring village," he remarked. "Which one was that?"

"Langham," she replied.

"I see. And I'm afraid I did not catch your name," he said.

"Ellen Burkard," she responded.

He eyed her curiously, unsure if he heard her correctly. "Did you say Burkard?"

"I did."

"And you mentioned your husband was named Sam," he said in a voice much more forceful than he had intended.

Mrs. Burkard swallowed slowly. "He was."

Colin paused, letting her words sink in. "Do you know what battalion he fought in?" he demanded.

She named his own unit, and added, "He was exceptionally proud of it."

Colin stared at the woman in disbelief, finding it hard to formulate words. "I have been looking for you, Mrs. Burkard."

She looked unsure. "May I ask why?"

"Your husband saved my life," Colin shared. "He gave up his own to ensure I had time to escape."

Tears came to Mrs. Burkard's eyes. "That sounds like my Sam. He was always looking out for other people."

Colin took a step closer to her. "It is my turn to return the favor," he said. "I want you to pack your belongings and I will send a coach to retrieve you."

"But where will we go?" Mrs. Burkard asked.

"You shall reside with me until we find you a more suitable place to live," Colin said.

"We can't possibly intrude—" Mrs. Burkard started.

"I'm afraid I won't take no for an answer," Colin asserted, holding up his hand. "You are now under my protection, and I refuse to let you live in squalor."

Peter grabbed his mother's arm. "Can you believe this is happening to us?"

Tears streamed down Mrs. Burkard's face. "I can scarcely believe it."

"You will not want for anything," Colin remarked. "I can promise you that."

"But, why?" Mrs. Burkard said. "You don't know us."

"No, but I knew Sam, and I know he would have wanted this for you and your son," Colin stated. "It is the least I can do for the man who gave his life for mine."

Mrs. Burkard nodded slowly. "I cannot thank you enough, milord."

"It is I who should be thanking you," Colin said, his voice growing emotional. "Now pack your things, or don't. It is entirely up to you, but a coach will be by shortly."

Colin glanced over at Arabella and gestured towards the door. "Shall we?"

As they exited the cottage, Arabella said, "That was rather unexpected."

"I have been looking for Sam Burkard's family since I arrived home," he explained as they walked towards the woodlands to collect their horses. "I just didn't expect to find them living right under my very nose."

With mirth in her eyes, she said, "You would have discovered them earlier if you had heeded my advice and become acquainted with your tenants."

A Tangled Wreath

Colin lifted his brow. "Are you truly gloating at a time like this?"

"I am," she replied. "Is there ever a bad time to gloat?"

He chuckled. "I suppose not."

"For whatever it is worth, I am glad that you found them," she said.

"As am I."

THE AFTERNOON SUN warmed his back as Colin penned a letter to the investigator. He felt as if a great weight had lifted off his shoulders now that he had found Sam Burkard's family. He would do whatever it took to ensure that he honored Sam's memory.

His mother walked into the room with a purposeful stride. "Do you want to explain to me why the guest bedrooms are being prepared?"

"I have invited Mrs. Burkard and her son to reside with us until I can find them a more adequate place to live."

"I'm afraid I am not acquainted with Mrs. Burkard."

"That doesn't surprise me. She used to work at the milliner's shop."

His mother gave him a blank stare. "Pray tell, why would you invite her into our home, as a guest, no less?"

Colin grew solemn as he shared, "Because she is the wife of the man who saved my life."

Her face softened as understanding dawned. "Then I shall treat this Mrs. Burkard and her son as our honored guests."

"Thank you, Mother."

"It is the least I can do."

Leaning back in his seat, he said, "I had been searching for Sam Burkard's relations since I arrived home, but I was fortunate to discover that Mrs. Burkard was one of my tenants."

"What do you intend to do with them?"

"The cottage they were renting is uninhabitable," Colin said. "I intend to gift them a cottage on our lands and see to it that Peter is properly educated."

"That is most generous of you."

Colin shook his head. "It is just a little thing."

"To you, perhaps, but you are changing their lives for the better."

He hesitated before saying, "There is one thing that I need your help with."

"Which is?"

"Mrs. Burkard does not have proof that she was wed, and I'm afraid the people in the village do not believe she is a respectable, married woman."

"How awful," his mother said. "That is why it is so important to safeguard the marriage lines."

"I agree, but there were some extenuating circumstances," he replied.

"Such as?"

"I'm afraid she lost the marriage lines in a fire. They barely escaped with their lives."

His mother came and sat down nearby. "Has she returned to the vestry and reviewed the parish register book?"

"The clerk has denied her that right."

"That is most unfortunate."

"I will not rest until I prove that Mrs. Burkard was properly married to her husband."

"And if you can't prove that?"

Colin shrugged. "It changes little for me."

"I can tell this is truly important to you."

"It is," he replied firmly.

"Then I will help with her reputation as much as I am able to."

"Thank you. That is precisely what I hoped you'd say."

A Tangled Wreath

His mother grew silent. "May I ask how Sam Burkard saved your life?"

Colin rose and walked over to the drink cart. As he picked up the decanter, he revealed, "We were assigned to fetch some documents from the enemy, but we were not as discreet as we had hoped." He poured himself a drink and replaced the decanter. "The alarm was sounded as we fled for our lives, but the French were right behind us."

He took a sip of his drink, then continued. "Sam sacrificed himself to the enemy to ensure I was able to escape."

His mother had tears in her eyes as she said, "I find myself immensely grateful to that man for allowing you to come home."

"I have a new purpose now," he shared. "I will care for Sam's family as if they were my own."

"I shall strive to do the same."

Colin placed his drink down on the tray. "For so long, I was angry that I was forced to come home, but now I am grateful that I was."

"Sometimes it may feel that the world is crashing down around us, but really it is just the pieces realigning themselves for our good."

Dickson stepped into the room and announced, "Mrs. Burkard and her son, Peter, have arrived, and are waiting in the drawing room."

"Wonderful," Colin replied. "Please remind the staff that they are to be treated with the utmost respect. If anyone fails to do so, they will be dismissed."

The butler tipped his head. "As you wish."

Colin assisted his mother in rising and said, "Mrs. Burkard will need a whole new wardrobe."

"I assumed as much."

They made their way towards the drawing room and stepped inside. Mrs. Burkard was now dressed in a faded yellow gown with a straw hat on her head. He assumed that she was wearing her finest dress for the occasion.

Mrs. Burkard curtsied, but her movements seemed stiff and awkward.

To his surprise, his mother approached Mrs. Burkard and embraced her warmly. "We are pleased to have you here," she said, leaning back.

Mrs. Burkard blinked. "Truly?"

His mother nodded. "My son told me about what your husband did, and I find him to be an honorable man."

"Thank you," Mrs. Burkard murmured, her eyes moist with tears.

Turning towards Peter, his mother said, "I assume this is your son."

"It is."

"We shall have to arrange riding lessons for him at once," his mother said.

Peter perked up. "I get to ride a horse?"

"That is, assuming you would like to."

With a bob of his head, Peter replied, "I would love to. I have been mucking up after them, but I haven't ever been able to ride one."

Colin interjected, "You will be able to ride as long as it does not interfere with your schooling."

"I get to go to school?" Peter asked in amazement.

"You do," Colin confirmed. "If your mother is agreeable, I intend to send you to a boarding school to prepare you for a life as a gentleman."

Mrs. Burkard shook her head. "This is all too much, milord," she said. "I wouldn't even be able to obtain employment in a fancy household such as this."

"I do not mean to make you uncomfortable," Colin remarked, "but you must accept that I intend to ensure that you will always be taken care of."

"We do not wish to be a burden."

A Tangled Wreath

Colin gave her a reassuring smile. "That is impossible, Mrs. Burkard."

His mother spoke up. "Did you bring your trunks with you?"

Mrs. Burkard lowered her gaze to the floor. "I'm afraid I don't own any trunks," she replied. "We don't have much in the way of material possessions."

"There is no shame in that," his mother responded. "It will save us the trouble of having to unpack."

Dickson stepped into the room. "The guest bedrooms have been readied, and I took the liberty of acquiring a maid to assist Mrs. Burkard."

"Thank you," his mother said. "That was most thoughtful of you."

Colin gestured towards the doorway. "Would you care to see your rooms?"

"I suppose so," Mrs. Burkard said, though she looked unsure.

Peter didn't share his mother's reservations; he was practically dancing on his toes. "I get my own room?"

"You do," Colin said.

"Does it have a bed?" Peter asked eagerly.

Amused, Colin replied, "It does."

"I'm hoping the straw will be dry in the mattress," Peter said. "I do not like sleeping on wet straw."

Colin's mother looked aghast. "You slept on a wet mattress?"

Peter nodded. "Our roof leaked, and the straw would soak up the water from the ground."

Colin clapped his hand on Peter's shoulder. "You will be sleeping on a feather mattress," he informed the boy.

"I can't wait to lay on it!" Peter paused. "Do you suppose my clothes will dirty the bed?"

"I wouldn't worry about that," Colin replied. "Besides, we have a tailor coming tomorrow to get you a whole new wardrobe."

"And I will see to a modiste for Mrs. Burkard," Colin's mother added.

Tears flowed down Mrs. Burkard's cheeks. "Thank you."

"Allow me to escort you to your bedchamber," his mother said. "Then I shall see to getting you a bath."

Peter groaned. "I hate baths," he declared. "The water is always so cold at the pond."

Colin chuckled. "The baths here are a much different experience, I can assure you of that."

As they walked out into the entry hall, Mrs. Burkard's eyes wandered over the walls with a sense of awe.

"I shall speak to Mr. Brown about acquiring a more suitable cottage for your needs," Colin remarked.

"I do hope it isn't too grand," Mrs. Burkard stated. "Peter and I don't need anything fancy. Just a roof above and a place to lay our heads."

"I shall see to it," Colin responded, "but until then, you are our honored guests."

He was pleased to see that Mrs. Burkard was beginning to accept her fortune, because he had only just begun to help them.

Chapter Seventeen

"Can you believe that Mrs. Burkard was under Colin's nose the entire time?" Arabella asked as she wiped the sides of her mouth with a linen napkin.

Her grandmother gave her an amused look. "I cannot."

"You should have seen the look on Mrs. Burkard's face when Colin said they were going to reside with him for the time being."

"I can only imagine."

"I am so happy for Mrs. Burkard and Peter," Arabella gushed. "Their cottage was truly horrific and did little to keep out the elements."

Reaching for her teacup, her grandmother remarked, "Perhaps we could speak of something else, since you have talked about little else since you got home yesterday."

Arabella recognized that her grandmother did have a point. "I do apologize, but I just find the whole thing fascinating."

"It does seem rather surreal."

"I agree," Arabella said. "After we left the cottage, Colin seemed different."

"In what way?"

"He seemed freer, lighter, somehow," she replied. "I know that may not make sense."

Her grandmother took a sip of her tea. "It makes perfect sense to me."

"I find what Colin is doing quite admirable."

"As do I." Her grandmother gave her a knowing look. "Has your opinion of Colin changed?"

"No," she replied. "He has just confirmed what I've always known."

"Which is?"

"He is the most honorable man that I know."

Her grandmother nodded. "I am pleased to hear that," she responded. "Does that mean you are ready to trust him with your heart again?"

Before Arabella could respond, Moore walked into the dining room and met her gaze. "You have a visitor, milady," he announced.

"Will you show Lord Barrett to the drawing room and inform him that I will be there in a moment?"

Moore shook his head. "You misunderstand me," he said. "Your father, Lord Clavering, has come to call."

"My father is here?" Arabella repeated in disbelief.

"Yes," Moore said. "He is in the drawing room and has requested a moment of your time."

She forced a smile to her lips. "Will you inform him that I will be there shortly?"

Moore tipped his head. "Yes, milady."

Her grandmother spoke up. "Would you care for me to accompany you?"

Arabella set her napkin on her plate. "That won't be necessary," she replied, rising, "but I do thank you for the offer."

"I wish you luck."

"Thank you," Arabella said as she headed towards the drawing room. She had no idea why her father had decided

A Tangled Wreath

to make the journey to visit her, but she was about to find out.

She stepped into the drawing room and saw that he was staring out the window. Her father was a tall man, with broad shoulders, and his dark hair had started turning white in some places.

"Father," she greeted.

He turned back around to face her, his expression unreadable. "Arabella," he said. "You are looking well."

"I do appreciate you for saying so."

"Did you have a pleasant Christmas?"

She nodded. "I did. May I ask how yours fared?"

"It was perfect," his father said. "Augusta informed me that she is increasing."

Arabella spoke through clenched teeth, hoping her words seemed cordial enough. "That is wonderful news."

"It is."

"Did you travel all this way to inform me of this news?"

Her father shifted in his stance. "I did not," he replied. "I came to talk to you about something much more serious."

"Which is?"

He gestured towards the settee. "Would you care to sit?"

Arabella walked over and sat down, clasping her hands in her lap.

Her father sat across from her. "Augusta and I heard the most distressing news a few days ago."

"What news was that?"

"Lord Eastwood came to our townhouse and informed us that you turned down his offer of marriage."

"I did," Arabella replied. "I have no desire to marry that man."

Her father looked displeased. "Why not?"

"Did you forget that he ran off with Lady Georgiana to Gretna Green?"

"I know, but his father stopped him from marrying her."

"Is that supposed to make it right?"

With a frown on his lips, his father said, "I daresay that most gentlemen of our station have some sort of sordid past."

"That is not true," Arabella replied. "I have met some honorable gentlemen."

"But none of those men are interested in you."

Her lips parted in surprise. "Pardon?"

"You have two broken engagements, and your future is uncertain unless you marry Lord Eastwood."

"I would rather remain a spinster than marry Lord Eastwood."

"And do what with your life?"

"I don't rightly know."

Her father shook his head. "You once had such a bright future, but you ruined it by showing favor to Lord Barrett."

"Why do you say that?"

"He was the second son of an earl and should have been beneath your notice," her father said. "Then he went and ruined you by breaking off your engagement."

"I am well aware," Arabella said curtly. "I do not need the reminder."

Her father met her gaze. "You don't know what I had to do to arrange for Lord Eastwood to offer for you."

"You arranged Lord Eastwood's offer for me?"

"I did," her father replied. "I had to agree to political favors with his father, in addition to a large sum of money."

"How much?"

"It doesn't matter—"

She spoke over him. "How much did you pay for Lord Eastwood to take me off your hands?"

Her father pursed his lips. "Ten thousand pounds."

Arabella sat back, stunned. "I can't believe you did that."

"You must understand that we were trying to help you."

"We?"

A Tangled Wreath

He nodded. "Yes, Augusta was worried about you, as well."

She huffed. "I truly doubt that."

"Why do you say that?"

"Augusta hates me," Arabella said, her voice rising.

"That is not true."

Arabella jumped up and declared, "Augusta has done everything in her power to ensure that I am uncomfortable in my own home."

"You are spouting nonsense."

"Why did she have me move bedchambers?" Arabella asked, placing a hand on her hip.

Her father shrugged. "She assumed you would be more comfortable in the other one."

"I think not."

"Regardless, Augusta and I are worried that you will become a spinster and be a drain on our household," her father said. "Marrying Lord Eastwood would solve that problem."

"It would, but you would be sentencing me to a life of unhappiness."

Her father sighed. "I daresay that you are being a bit dramatic. All marriages have some strife."

"I refuse to marry Lord Eastwood."

"I was hoping you would be reasonable," he said. "After all, I traveled all the way from London to personally speak to you about this."

Arabella dropped her hand. "This conversation could have waited until I returned home."

"I'm afraid it couldn't wait."

"Why is that?"

Her father looked uncomfortable as he remarked, "If you are not willing to marry Lord Eastwood, then it will be best if you retired to our country estate."

"For how long?"

He hesitated before asking, "I don't believe there is a purpose for you to return to London, do you?"

Her mouth dropped. "You are banishing me to our country estate?"

"No sensible man will want you now that you have two broken engagements, despite your generous dowry."

"I can't believe you are doing this to me."

"Augusta and I feel that it would be best for you to be in your own household—"

She cut him off, attempting to keep the hurt out of her voice. "This is all because of Augusta."

"No, it is not," he replied. "We came to this decision together."

Crossing her arms over her chest, she asked, "What would Mother think of you banishing me to a life in the country?"

A pained look came to his face. "That is not fair of you," he stated. "You created this mess, and now you have to deal with the consequences."

"I did no such thing!"

"I'm beginning to wonder if you even know what you want in this life."

An image of Colin came to her mind, and she didn't hesitate to reply, "I know precisely what I want."

"And what is that?" his father asked, his voice skeptical.

She tilted her chin. "I want to marry Lord Barrett."

Her father scoffed. "Did you forget that Lord Barrett does not want to marry you?"

As she opened her mouth to reply, Colin's voice came from the doorway. "Do you mean that, Bella?"

COLIN KNEW that he shouldn't have been eavesdropping, but he'd heard the pain in Arabella's voice, drawing him in. He'd been about to make his presence known when she'd

A Tangled Wreath

said it, the most wonderful thing, and he could scarcely believe it. She had informed her father that she wished to marry him.

Her words had shaken Colin to the very core, causing him to make a most awkward entrance. Now he just stood there, waiting for her to answer, and the silence was deafening.

Arabella turned to face him, openly surprised. "Colin! I hadn't realized you'd arrived."

Colin stepped further into the room, but his eyes never strayed from hers. "Did you mean what you said?"

Her eyes darted towards her father. "I did."

Before Colin could respond, Lord Clavering spoke up. "Absolutely not!" he exclaimed. "I forbid a union between you two."

Arabella arched an eyebrow. "You forbid it?"

Lord Clavering nodded. "I do," he replied. "Lord Barrett is an earl, but Lord Eastwood will one day be a marquess; a wealthy one, at that."

"I have already told you that I have no intention of marrying Lord Eastwood," Arabella said.

"Your reasons are foolhardy," Lord Clavering stated, waving his hand dismissively in front of him. "Regardless, did you not forget that Lord Barrett broke your engagement, just as Lord Eastwood did?"

"Lord Eastwood fled to Gretna Green with another woman," Arabella remarked. "It is hardly the same thing."

Lord Clavering's critical eye swept over Colin before asking, "How do I know you won't hurt Arabella again?"

"You have my word," Colin replied.

Lord Clavering huffed. "That means little to me."

"Why is that?"

"Because of you, my daughter's reputation was tarnished amongst the *ton*," Lord Clavering said. "She wasn't received well at certain social gatherings."

"I am well aware, and I intend to do right by her."

Lord Clavering crossed his arms over his chest. "By marrying her?"

"Yes," Colin replied, "assuming she truly will have me."

With a shake of his head, Lord Clavering turned back towards his daughter. "I would prefer it if you married Lord Eastwood."

Arabella rose. "Why is that?"

"Lord Eastwood would be able to give you a life that you could only dream about," Lord Clavering said. "His father is one of the richest landowners in all of England."

"He is also a despicable lout," Arabella remarked. "He intends to maintain his mistress, even after being wed."

Her father frowned. "I had not realized that."

"He is not the type of man I wish to marry."

"But Lord Barrett is?"

Arabella snuck a glance at Colin. "He is."

Lord Clavering stood there for a long moment, his expression stoic. "I am not pleased by this, but I won't stand in your way."

"Thank you, Father," Arabella said.

Lord Clavering uncrossed his arms and shifted his gaze to Colin. "You have disappointed me once. Try not to make a habit out of it."

"No, sir," Colin said.

"I must assume that you two have much to discuss, so I will step out for a moment," Lord Clavering stated as he walked over to the door. "Say what needs to be said, and do not dally."

After Lord Clavering departed, Colin brought his attention back towards Arabella. "Your father was right; we do have a lot to discuss."

"That we do."

"Where should we start?" he asked, taking a step closer to her.

Arabella gave him a timid smile. "I don't rightly know."

"Perhaps we should start with the fact that you said you wanted to marry me."

"I would prefer not to."

"Why is that?"

She clasped her hands in front of her. "It was rather bold of me to say such a thing."

Colin smiled. "I found it rather refreshing and forthright," he said. "Quite frankly, I would prefer honesty between us."

"I would like that, as well."

"Then I shall start." He paused. "I have never stopped loving you these past five years; if anything, my love for you has increased. When I sleep, I dream of you, and when I wake, I long to hold you in my arms."

Arabella's breath hitched. "Is that so?"

"I was a fool to think I could live my life without you," Colin said. "I know you may not need me in your life, but I need you in mine, desperately."

She took a tentative step towards him. "I do need you in my life, now more than ever."

"I know you are scared—"

Arabella spoke over him. "Not anymore."

"No?"

"When I saw you at the cottage with Mrs. Burkard and Peter, I remembered why I originally fell in love with you," she said.

"Which was?"

"You are an honorable man with a compassionate heart."

Colin closed the distance between them. "May I presume that you still hold me in some regard, then?"

"I love you, Colin," she said with a smile. "I have always loved you, even when I hated you."

"I know I did not make this easy on us, but our time apart has only made me more certain that I want to spend the rest of my life with you."

"I feel the same way."

Colin reached for her hand. "Does this mean you will marry me?"

"You must say it properly," Arabella said. "I won't answer unless you kneel down and everything."

Colin gave her an amused look as he bent down onto one knee. "Lady Arabella Wyndham, will you do me the grand honor of becoming my wife?"

"Yes," Arabella breathed.

Rising, he asked, "Do I dare kiss you with your father in the next room over?"

Arabella gave him a coy smile. "It is a risk I am willing to take."

"You are so beautiful," Colin said as he leaned closer.

He didn't wait for her response before he pressed his mouth to hers, softly but firmly. Then he moved one arm around her waist and pulled her closer to him. This kiss was different than the one in the woods had been; this one was filled with promise.

Colin was so distracted that he barely heard Lord Clavering exclaim, "Release my daughter!"

He broke the kiss and dropped his arm but remained close. He turned towards Lord Clavering, who had a thunderous look on his face.

"Your daughter has agreed to marry me," Colin informed him.

"That still doesn't give you the right to kiss her so brazenly," Lord Clavering asserted

"Don't be so prudish, Father," Arabella said.

Lord Clavering shot her a disapproving look. "I see that your grandmother has been wearing off on you."

"That she has," Arabella confirmed.

As if on cue, Lady Langdon stepped into the drawing room. "Are congratulations in order?" she asked.

Arabella bobbed her head. "They are."

Lady Langdon clasped her hands together. "That is

wonderful news!" she exclaimed. "This is precisely the outcome that I was hoping for."

Lord Clavering lifted his brow. "Dare I assume that you plied your hand at matchmaking?"

"I did, and it worked splendidly," Lady Langdon said. "It was obvious that they belonged with one another."

"Well, I, for one, thank you for your assistance," Colin interjected. "Without your help, it might have been impossible to convince Arabella to marry me."

"Your mother helped, as well," Lady Langdon shared.

"That does not surprise me in the least," Colin said.

Lord Clavering turned his attention towards his daughter. "It would be best if you return to London with me until the banns have been posted."

Arabella glanced at him. "I would prefer to stay here."

"Absolutely not!" Lord Clavering shouted. "I can't trust that you will be properly chaperoned."

"Grandmother has been an exemplary chaperone," Arabella argued.

Lord Clavering huffed. "I truly doubt that. I'm surprised she hasn't been following you around holding that blasted mistletoe over your heads."

Colin spoke up. "Would it ease your mind if I went and acquired a special license from Town?" he asked. "That way we could be married at once."

"It would," Lord Clavering said.

Turning towards her, Colin asked, "Is this acceptable to you?"

"I would marry you today, tomorrow, or any day thereafter," Arabella said. "I just never want to let you go."

"I can assure you that the feeling is mutual," he replied. "It might be best if I depart for London, then."

"That would be wise."

He leaned in and kissed her on her cheek, his lips lingering. "I shall not be long," he murmured.

"I will be here, waiting for your return."

Lord Clavering cleared his throat. "I believe you have properly said your goodbyes," he scoffed. "You are going to be gone for a day, not going to war."

Colin stepped back from Arabella. "I promise that I will return to you."

"See that you do."

Dear Margarette

Langdon Hall, Maidstone
December 30, 1815

I daresay that you have missed the most exciting Christmas, and I can barely contain my excitement as I write this letter. I have succeeded! Colin and Arabella finally set aside their differences and are to be married today. Can you believe that?

But their journey was not an easy one. Do you remember how Lord Eastwood and Arabella were previously engaged? He traveled to Langdon Hall to try to persuade her to marry him... again. Fortunately, my granddaughter rejected his proposal and sent him on his way. I do not care for that man. He aggravated me from the moment he stepped foot into the drawing room.

It wasn't long before Arabella's father, Lord Clavering, showed up to try to convince her to marry Lord Eastwood. I was proud of Arabella because she stood her ground against her father. During this time, Colin arrived at Langdon Hall and declared his love for Arabella.

It was a sweet moment, one that I eavesdropped on. I

know you would be terribly disappointed in me, but I couldn't resist.

This Christmas was anything but ordinary, and I didn't even tell you about the poacher that was found on Colin's land. That is a story that will need to be told in person, which I hope will be soon. I can't wait to hear about your matchmaking attempts, and I am hoping you were successful, as well.

Now that I have set out what I intended to do, I find that I need a holiday. It is exhausting being a matchmaker.

Yours fondly,
Esther

Chapter Eighteen

Colin stared out the window of his bedchamber, not quite believing that this day had finally arrived. It had been three days since he had secured the special license, and he had hardly seen Arabella during that time. But that was about to change, because today was his wedding day. In a few hours, he would never have to be apart from her again.

His valet spoke up from behind him. "White or ivory?"

Colin turned to face him. "White."

"You are being rather decisive today, milord," Simon joked as he extended the white cravat towards him. "That bodes well for the future Lady Barrett."

Colin accepted the cravat and walked over to the mirror. As he was tying the intricate knot, he said, "Today is going to be a marvelous day."

"Yes, it is," Simon agreed.

"I can't help but wonder how radically different my life would have been had my brother not passed away."

"That is a most distasteful thought."

"It is, but I doubt I would have ever won Arabella's hand in marriage if I was still serving in the army."

"You do not know that," Simon replied. "Fate has a peculiar way of intervening in people's lives."

"That it does," Colin agreed, walking over to the door.

"I wish you luck, milord," Simon said.

"Will you be at the wedding?"

Simon smiled. "I would not miss it."

Colin departed out of his room and started walking down the hall. As he reached the top of the stairs, he saw his brother coming from the other direction.

John held his arms out wide. "There he is," he remarked enthusiastically. "The bridegroom."

"It is only a few weeks until you are to be wed yourself."

"Who would have thought that you would beat me to the altar?" John asked.

Colin shook his head. "Not me."

"But I am glad that you did so."

With a smile, Colin said, "I do appreciate you coming to my wedding, especially since it was such short notice."

"When you rode into Town in a blaze to secure a special license, I knew I had no choice but to make the trek back up here again."

"It will be nice to have you standing up with me."

John gave him a knowing look. "You will be returning the favor shortly."

"Yes, I will."

As they started descending the stairs, John asked, "Do you intend to take a wedding tour?"

"I intend to abscond with Arabella the moment she says yes."

John chuckled. "I daresay Mother would never forgive you if you missed the luncheon she has prepared in your honor."

His mother's voice came from the bottom of the stairs. "John is right," she said. "I would be very angry with you if you did such a thing."

Colin came to a stop in front of his mother. "You do not

need to fret. We will stay for the luncheon, but we will depart shortly thereafter for our Scottish manor."

"You seem to be rather eager to get Arabella alone," John teased.

His mother swatted at John's sleeve. "We do not talk of such things," she chided lightly. "What happens between a man and a woman is their business."

John smirked. "How does the bridegroom wish to spend his last few hours of freedom?"

"Work," Colin replied.

"That is so drab and boring," John said. "Why don't we go into the village and drink at the pub? We haven't done that in years."

"Yes, and I remember the last time we went, we became so inebriated that we were barely able to make it back home."

John chuckled. "That was a memorable evening."

"But the next morning was miserable."

"That it was," John agreed.

Before he could reply, Peter ran into the entry hall with a kite in his hand. "Look what Dickson just made for me," he shouted, holding it up with pride.

"It is impressive," John said. "It is much more impressive than the ones that Dickson used to make for me when I was little."

Dickson chuckled as he walked into the room. "I have had a lot more time to practice since then, sir."

"Mother said I can't fly it until after the wedding," Peter said, his voice resigned.

Colin placed his hand on the boy's thin shoulder. "You have a wise mother."

"That I do," Peter agreed. "Although, she does believe you spoil me terribly."

"It is the least I can do," Colin replied.

Dickson caught his eye and informed him, "Mr. Hardwick is waiting for you in your study."

"Thank you," Colin said. "If you will all excuse me, I need to speak to my solicitor for a moment."

His mother sighed. "But it is your wedding day, son," she said. "I would prefer if you took the day off."

"I'm afraid this can't wait," Colin asserted.

With a disapproving glance, his mother replied, "Then off you go, but I won't let you be late to your own wedding."

"Heaven forbid," Colin said as he walked towards his study.

Once he stepped inside, he saw his solicitor already seated in front of the desk, reviewing a document in his hand. Mr. Hardwick was a round man with a full head of red hair and had been with his family for many years.

"Good morning, Mr. Hardwick," Colin greeted as he came around his desk. "Thank you for coming so early."

"It was the least I could do for my favorite client," Mr. Hardwick said, smiling. "Besides, I believe congratulations are in order."

"That is only if she says yes."

Mr. Hardwick's smile dimmed. "Pardon?"

"I am teasing," Colin said, taking his seat. "Forgive me; I'm afraid it is a little wedding humor."

With a chuckle, Mr. Hardwick remarked, "You are in a pleasant mood for a man who is about to get caught by the parson's mousetrap."

"Why wouldn't I be?" Colin asked. "I fought hard to convince Lady Arabella to marry me."

"The good ones usually need more convincing."

"Well said, Mr. Hardwick."

The solicitor extended the paper he had been holding towards Colin. "This may put you into an even better mood, if that is at all possible."

"What is it?" Colin asked as he accepted the paper.

"It is the marriage lines for Mr. and Mrs. Burkard," Mr. Hardwick revealed.

Colin stared at the document in disbelief. "How were you able to acquire it?"

"It was quite simple," Mr. Hardwick smiled, "once I threatened to refer the matter over to the magistrate."

"Perhaps you should start at the beginning," Colin said, putting the document down.

"I visited Langham and went to the vestry to see the parish register book," Mr. Hardwick started. "But the parish clerk was being rather unreasonable when I explained my purpose for being there."

"Why was that?"

"He said he did not remember attending a wedding on the date in question and that I should let the matter drop," Mr. Hardwick revealed. "But it all changed once I explained that I was your solicitor, and you were deeply vested in finding the truth."

"How did he respond to that?"

"His face grew white, and he shut the door on my face," Mr. Hardwick shared. "But that did little to deter me."

"I am pleased to hear that, considering what I am paying you."

Mr. Hardwick grinned. "I went around back and found an unlocked door. I entered the vestry and found the parish clerk rifling through a book. When he saw me, he slammed the book shut and held it behind him." He paused. "That is when I threatened to refer the matter to the magistrate, and he relented rather quickly thereafter."

The solicitor shifted in his seat, then continued. "Apparently, Mrs. Burkard's father paid the parish clerk some money to not release the book to his daughter, casting her marital status into question."

"How awful," Colin said.

"I was informed that Mrs. Burkard's father is not known for his scrupulous business dealings in the village," Mr. Hardwick remarked.

"That is most unfortunate, but not unexpected." Mr. Hardwick pointed at the marriage lines. "The document is missing a few signatures, but this should provide enough proof that she was indeed married, as she claimed to be."

"I never doubted her."

"And if anyone else does question the validity of the marriage, they can review the parish register book themselves."

"I don't believe it will come down to that, not anymore," Colin said. "Mrs. Burkard and her son will remain under my protection, and I dare anyone to try to disparage them."

Mr. Hardwick nodded. "Mrs. Burkard is a lucky woman to have such a fierce protector as yourself."

"It is the least I can do."

Mr. Hardwick reached into his satchel and pulled out another sheet of paper. "I also have the deed for the Cosworth cottage, and I have transferred it to Mrs. Burkard, per your request," he said, extending the paper.

"Thank you." Colin's eyes reviewed the deed. "I do appreciate how quickly you work."

"As I said, you are my favorite client," Mr. Hardwick said. "It also helps that my wife took our children to visit her parents this past week."

Colin rose and put his hand out for the deed. "I have no doubt that Mrs. Burkard will be pleased with the Cosworth cottage."

"I would imagine that to be the case," Mr. Hardwick said, rising. "If you need anything else, please do not hesitate to send for me."

After the solicitor left the room, Colin sat back down, and a smile came to his lips. The Cosworths' cottage was far enough way to grant Mrs. Burkard and her son privacy, but close enough that he could ensure they were taken care of. He had accomplished what he had set out to do, and it felt wonderful.

ARABELLA STARED out the window of the coach, admiring the passing countryside and avoiding conversation with her father and stepmother across from her. They'd arrived the day before and had spent the time since criticizing her decision to marry Colin. Frankly, little else needed to be said between them.

Her father's voice drew her attention. "It is a lovely day for a wedding."

"I find the weather to be rather drab today," Augusta remarked.

Arabella took a moment to study her stepmother. She had blonde hair, a thin face, and a large nose. She wasn't entirely unfortunate to look at, but she was not the beauty Arabella's mother had been. However, it was her shrill voice that had always grated on the nerves.

"I do worry that the *ton* will gossip about how quickly you are marrying after breaking your engagement with Lord Eastwood," Augusta said.

"Lord Eastwood broke the engagement, not me," Arabella reminded her. "I'm sure the *ton* will understand, since he ran off to Gretna Green with Lady Georgiana."

Augusta sighed dramatically. "I do hope your actions do not affect our place amongst the Beau Monde."

"Colin and I only intend to spend time in Town during the Season," Arabella remarked.

"That is a relief," Augusta said. "With any luck, the *ton* will move onto another scandal and forget about you and your rush to the altar."

"I wouldn't say that I am rushing to the altar."

"Aren't you?" Augusta questioned, arching her thin

eyebrow. "Why not just post the banns and wait three weeks' time?"

"Colin did not wish to wait that long."

"Patience is a virtue," Augusta stated. "The *ton* is not kind to people who acquire special licenses."

"Why is that?"

"It makes people wonder if there were some extenuating circumstances that required you to marry right away."

"Such as?"

Augusta placed a hand on her stomach. "One might wonder if you are increasing."

Arabella's lips parted in disbelief. "I am not increasing!" she said, her voice rising. "How can you even insinuate that?"

"It isn't what I'm thinking, but the *ton*."

Her father cleared his throat. "I do believe you have made your point, Augusta."

A smug smile tugged at her stepmother's lips. "I was merely informing Arabella of the repercussions of her actions."

"Today should be one of felicitations, and we shouldn't spend our remaining moments with her by chastising her," her father remarked.

Augusta nodded. "You are right," she said. "It would be terrible of us to remind Arabella that she is settling by marrying Lord Barrett."

"That it would," her father responded.

The coach came to a stop in front of the church, and it dipped to the side as the footman stepped off his perch.

Once the door was opened, her father turned towards Augusta and asked, "Would you mind if I had a moment alone with Arabella?"

A displeased look came to Augusta's face. "You just want me to wait outside for you?"

"You could always step into the church and wait at one of the pews," her father suggested. "I will be along shortly."

A Tangled Wreath

"See that you are. I do not like to be kept waiting," Augusta murmured as she exited the coach.

Her father reached for the door and closed it. "I would like for this conversation to remain private," he said.

Arabella gave him an expectant look, unsure of what he wished to speak about. She truly hoped he didn't intend to continue to reprimand her for marrying Colin.

Her father's eyes grew reflective. "You look just like your mother did on our wedding day," he said. "Your beauty will outshine all others."

"Thank you, Father," she responded, pleased by his remarks.

He cocked his head. "Are you happy?"

"I am," she replied. "I have been in love with Colin since I first laid eyes on him."

"I'm pleased to hear that."

"I know you may not understand my reasons for marrying Colin, but I can assure you that he is my love match, in every sense of the word."

Her father smiled sadly. "I had that with your mother," he said softly. "She was the love of my life."

Feeling bold, Arabella asked, "If that is the case, why did you marry Augusta so soon after Mother died?"

Tears came to his eyes and his voice was choked with emotion. "I was lonely, lost, and I thought a companion would fill the empty void in my heart."

"Did it?"

"No," he replied. "It is still there, and I suspect it will always be there."

"I understand that feeling well."

Her father blinked back his tears. "I know it hasn't been easy for you to have Augusta as your stepmother, but I will speak to her about her sharp tongue."

"I daresay that it won't make any difference."

"Why is that?"

Arabella gave him a pointed look. "You and I used to be close, but Augusta is determined to drive a wedge between us."

"That is not true," he responded. "She is just trying to adjust to her new role as the mistress of the house."

"When was the last time we went riding together?" Arabella asked.

Her father winced. "It has been some time, but Augusta prefers that we have breakfast together."

"Do you remember how I used to read to you in the library after dinner?"

"I do," he replied. "Those moments were very special to me."

"Yet you stopped coming to the library after you wed Augusta."

He frowned. "Augusta does not like being apart from me."

"I miss you, Father," she said. "Sometimes I feel as if I lost both parents the day that Mother died."

Leaning forward, her father reached for her hand. "I am still here, and you will never lose me," he asserted. "I can promise you that."

Arabella felt tears prick at the back of her eyes. "I am happy to hear you say that, but I worry if that is true."

"I can assure you that things will change once we arrive back in London," her father said. "I believe it is time that I put Augusta in her place."

"That won't be easy."

Her father gave her a tender smile. "But it will be worth it." He paused. "I'm sorry I have been vocal about my disapproval of Lord Barrett, but I just want you to be sure of your choice."

"I am, wholeheartedly."

"Then I shall support your decision, and I will welcome Lord Barrett into the family."

"Thank you," she murmured as a tear rolled down her cheek.

Her father reached forward and wiped it away. "You mustn't cry on your wedding day. What would Lord Barrett think?"

"These are happy tears," Arabella assured him.

"Your mother used to cry when she was happy, as well," her father remarked, his voice soft. "And I have no doubt she would be crying at this very moment, if she were here."

"I miss her so much."

Her father nodded. "As do I," he said. "I would give up all that I have if I could just see her for a moment."

"I feel the same way."

A smile came to his lips, but it didn't reach his eyes. "Are you ready?" he asked.

"I am."

Her father released her hand and opened the door. After he stepped out, he stretched forth his hand to help her out of the coach.

Arabella exited the coach and stared up at the church. There was no doubt in her heart about marrying Colin. She loved him, more than anything else in the whole world.

"Shall we go inside?" her father asked as he placed her hand in the crook of his arm.

"Yes," she replied.

As they walked towards the doors, Arabella felt a fluttering in her stomach at the thought of seeing Colin. She hadn't seen him much these past few days, and she missed him. She wondered if she would always react that way to him.

Her father opened the door and stood to the side as she entered. To her surprise, not only were the pews decorated with flowers, but they were filled with people from the village.

"I thought this was to be a small wedding," her father whispered to her.

"As did I."

Her eyes roamed over the church until they landed on Colin. He was staring at her with an intensity that she had never seen before, causing her breath to hitch. This was the man she loved, and it was evident by the way he was staring that he loved her, as well.

Slowly, they made their way to the front of the church, Arabella's eyes not straying from Colin. There was no other place she wished to look. It was just him and her, nothing else mattered.

Her father took her hand and extended it towards Colin, who readily accepted it. Once she was standing next to him, her fiancé leaned closer and whispered, "You look so beautiful, Bella."

"Thank you," she murmured.

The vicar began the ceremony, and she attempted to concentrate on what was being said, but it was growing increasingly difficult to do so. All she could think about was how she was about to become Colin's wife, and she found herself smiling at that thought.

Everything that she had been forced to endure over the years had led her to this moment. This perfect moment, with the perfect man for her. It had been worth it.

Epilogue

Six years later

COLIN CARRIED HIS SON, James, on his shoulder as he walked along the path through the woodlands. He glanced back and saw Arabella and their daughter, Esther, trailing behind, chatting merrily.

"What about that tree, Father?" his son asked, pointing at a large pine tree.

"That would make an impressive tree, but I have my eye on something bigger," he responded.

Arabella's voice came from behind him. "I pray that isn't so," she said. "Last year, your tree barely fit through the door of the saloon."

"I have since learned my lesson," Colin remarked.

Esther spoke up. "Why do we always pick two trees for the saloon?"

"That is an interesting story," Arabella said. "I am sure that your father would like to tell you the reasons behind it."

"I would." Colin came to a stop and turned back around to face his daughter. "A long, long time ago, before your mother and I were married, we were assigned to pick out a tree for Christmas," he explained. "We went deep into the forest to select the perfect tree and your mother picked out a sad-looking pine that frightened children."

Esther's eyes grew wide. "It frightened children?"

Arabella smiled. "No, it most definitely did not," she replied. "Your father is just making up stories again."

"The tree may not have scared children, but it made them sad," Colin corrected.

"Is that true, Mother?" James asked.

Arabella shook her head. "The tree did not make any children sad, but it was rather unfortunate-looking."

"Why did you select that one, then?" Esther asked.

"I thought it had a lot of character," Arabella said. "It tried its hardest to be a tree, and I thought it should be rewarded for that."

Esther bobbed her head. "That was nice of you."

"Thank you," Arabella replied.

"Is that why you pick out small, feeble trees and Father picks the grandest trees?" Esther asked innocently.

"I pick out whatever tree speaks to me," Arabella said.

Esther stared at her. "Trees can speak to you?" she asked. "What do they say?"

"Mostly they just talk about how much they want to be a part of our Christmas festivities," Arabella replied.

With pressed lips, Esther inquired, "Are you making up stories, as well?"

"I am," Arabella confirmed.

Colin lifted James off his shoulder and set him gently on the ground. "Come, I believe I found the perfect tree for this year," he encouraged.

He led them further down the path and stopped at a glorious pine tree. He put his hands out wide and asked, "What do you think?"

Arabella tilted her head up and replied, "This has to be at least twelve feet tall."

"That shouldn't be a problem," Colin replied, admiring the long, protruding branches. "We can cut the top off to make it fit in the saloon."

Arabella looked hesitant. "That doesn't seem like a good idea."

"It will work," he said, reaching into his pocket to pull out a red ribbon. "You must trust me on this."

"All right," she conceded. "But this only proves how much I love you."

After he'd secured the ribbon to the tree, he turned his attention back to his wife. "Has any tree spoken to you yet?" he teased.

Her eyes left his and roamed the woodlands. "Not yet," she replied. "Perhaps we should let the children decide this year."

Esther clasped her hands together. "Do you mean it?"

"I do," Arabella replied. "Why don't you and James pick out a tree?"

Reaching for her brother's hand, Esther said, "We will find a tree that doesn't make anyone sad."

Colin watched as his children roamed the woods and found himself beaming with pride. "I love watching our children play together."

"It is rare for them to be playing nicely, and not fighting."

"They do seem to fight constantly, but I was that way with my brothers growing up."

Arabella started walking down the path as the children headed further into the woodlands. "I am pleased that Peter and his mother will be joining us for our Christmas festivities this year."

"I agree," Colin replied. "We haven't seen much of Peter since he started at Cambridge."

"He has grown into a remarkable man."

"That he has," Colin agreed. "I know he has grand plans to become a barrister."

Arabella reached for his hand. "He is certainly smart enough."

Glancing over at her, he asked, "Is your father coming for Christmas?"

"I believe so," she replied. "Although, it might be hard for Augusta to travel in a coach for too long."

"She always seems to be increasing."

Arabella giggled. "That she does, and Father is beside himself," she said. "He has four children under the age of seven."

"I hope he is happy."

"He appears to be."

Colin stopped and turned to face her. "Are you happy?"

She smiled. "Blissfully so."

"That warms my heart to hear," he said, leaning closer. "I am a smart enough man to know that I need to keep my wife happy if I ever want to kiss her."

"You always have my permission to kiss me."

Colin pressed his lips against hers and wrapped his arms around her waist. As he pulled her closer, he heard Esther's voice in the distance.

"We found a tree!"

He reluctantly released his wife and leaned back. "Duty calls."

They hurried over to where Esther and James were standing, and they were proudly gesturing at a small pine tree.

Esther stepped forward and declared, "We have found a tree that is better than yours, Father."

"Is that so?" he asked, amused.

James bobbed his head. "It's bigger than me."

"That it is, but not much bigger than Esther," Colin said. "We could always keep searching and find something bigger."

"We don't want something bigger," Esther responded. "This tree spoke to me and told us to take it home."

Colin chuckled. "It spoke to you?"

Esther smiled widely, revealing her two missing teeth. "I can speak to trees, just like Mother."

Reaching into his pocket, Colin removed another red ribbon and tied it to one of the branches. "If this is the tree that you want, then who am I to judge?"

Arabella nudged his shoulder with hers. "You give in much too easily to them," she said.

"I do," he readily admitted. "I have a soft spot for them, and for you."

"That you do."

Reaching down, he picked up James and returned him to his place atop his shoulders. "Shall we return home and get some chocolate for our efforts here today?"

"I love chocolate!" Esther declared.

Colin held his hand out for her. "I know," he replied. "That is why I suggested it."

As they walked back to the manor, Colin marveled that his heart was so full. He had been blessed with a loving wife, two beautiful children, and an estate that was immensely profitable. He had once thought it wasn't fair of him to survive the war when others hadn't, but he had come to recognize that he must show his gratitude by living his life the best way that he could.

The End

Next in A Christmas Match Series
A Wish for Father Christmas by Laura Rollins

A Christmas Match Series*

A Wish for Father Christmas
By Laura Rollins

A Sleighride Kiss
By Jen Geigle Johnson

A Yorkshire Carol
By Jennie Goutet

A Mistletoe Mistletoe Mismatch
By Sally Britton

A Tangled Wreath
By Laura Beers

*Books in this series may be read in any order

Also by Laura Beers

Proper Regency Matchmakers

Saving Lord Berkshire

Reforming the Duke

Loving Lord Egleton

Redeeming the Marquess

Engaging Lord Charles

Refining Lord Preston (coming Feb 2022)

Regency Spies & Secrets

A Dangerous Pursuit

A Dangerous Game

A Dangerous Lord

A Dangerous Scheme

Regency Brides: A Promise of Love

A Clever Alliance

The Reluctant Guardian

A Noble Pursuit

The Earl's Daughter

A Foolish Game

The Beckett Files

Saving Shadow

A Peculiar Courtship

To Love a Spy

A Tangled Ruse
A Deceptive Bargain
The Baron's Daughter
The Unfortunate Debutante

About the Author

Laura Beers is an award-winning author. She attended Brigham Young University, earning a Bachelor of Science degree in Construction Management. She can't sing, doesn't dance and loves naps.

Besides being a full-time homemaker to her three kids, she loves waterskiing, hiking, and drinking Dr. Pepper. She was born and raised in Southern California, but she now resides in South Carolina.

Made in the USA
Monee, IL
27 November 2024